Also by Mary Beckett
Give Them Stones

A BELFAST WOMAN

STORIES BY

Mary Beckett

William Morrow and Company, Inc.
New York

Copyright © 1980 by Mary Beckett

A Belfast Woman was first published by Poolbeg Press Ltd., Dublin.

All rights reserved. No part of this book may be reproduced or utilized in any form or by any means, electronic or mechanical, including photocopying, recording or by any information storage and retrieval system, without permission in writing from the Publisher. Inquiries should be addressed to Permissions Department, William Morrow and Company, Inc., 105 Madison Ave., New York, N.Y. 10016.

Library of Congress Cataloging-in-Publication Data

Beckett, Mary, 1926–
A Belfast woman : stories / by Mary Beckett.
p. cm.
ISBN 0-688-08221-1
I. Title.
PR6052.E284B45 1989
823'.914—dc19   88-25975
                                                                                        CIP

Printed in the United States of America

First U.S. Edition

1 2 3 4 5 6 7 8 9 10

BOOK DESIGN BY WILLIAM MCCARTHY

For Sister Mary Laurentia,
O.P., Belfast

Contents

A BELFAST
WOMAN

The Excursion

All evening Eleanor could think of nothing but the excursion. The women had been talking about it in the shop that day. The Young Farmers Club was running an excursion to Dublin and most of the women were going, but it hadn't occurred to Eleanor that it was possible for her to go till next morning. And the excursion was tomorrow. That didn't leave much time. If she wanted to go at all, she would have to ask James at teatime.

She hated the thought of asking James. It wasn't that they couldn't afford the money. It was only on account of his money that she had married him at all. And what good had it ever done her? When she married James she had great plans to do wonderful things with his wealth. That was her father's fault. He had always kept on say-

ing, "Money's power, me girl, money's power!" Well, here she was with plenty of money that she didn't seem to be able to spend—money she had saved for the children who had never come, for the fine new house that James had refused to put up. Plenty of money and she couldn't even go on an excursion without asking him.

He would look so surprised, the way he had done when she wanted to go for a week to Warrenpoint with her cousin Sarah. He hadn't said no but he had been so astonished that she couldn't face his continued exclamations and had told him she wouldn't go after all. But this time she *would* go. It was for only one day and he could do without her quite well.

It would be perfect just to sit back in the train passing fields of crops she needn't worry about and lines of washing someone else had done. And then in Dublin she would have a whole day to look at the shops. Somehow, when she went to Belfast she never seemed to have time to see anyplace except the market and the bus station. She had never been in Dublin and had never been able to join in conversation with other women discussing the curtains and the delft and the wallpaper they could bring home. She had to stay quiet all the time they talked about what the Customs men said and did. But after tomorrow all that would be different.

She heard James's step in the yard and hurried to set the table for the tea; he was always rushing to go out again. He came in and sat down at the table, throwing his cap down on the floor beside him. He began to eat at once, without speaking, and ate steadily on. Eleanor's mouth grew drier and drier and she reminded herself that if she did not speak soon he would be away out again.

Then James raised his head and said, "Did you hear

about the excursion to Dublin?" And then he put another piece of bread in his mouth and began to chew. Her heart started to beat with slow, heavy thumps. Maybe he would tell her she should go. But he had never done such a thing—it wasn't possible. She became impatient. Why wouldn't he finish what he had to say? It flashed into her mind that she usually hadn't the slightest interest in what he would say. "I was thinking of going," James said then.

The room was very still. It was hot and the air was heavy. Her heart began to beat normally again. She knew all the time that she would never have managed to go. All the bitterness and the fierce determination of the afternoon ebbed out of her and she acquiesced dully. "I suppose you might as well." James rose and went out.

Eleanor sat at the table for a long time then, just sitting. Presently she got up and began to clear away the tea things with slow, ponderous movements, as if she had used all her energy in making up her mind to ask James about the excursion. Then she began to be angry with herself. Where was the use of going on like this? Hadn't she known all along at the back of her mind that it wouldn't work out right? Sure it never did and she was only making a fool of herself pretending that it would. All those dreams that she had were nonsense—wasting her time imagining foolishness like that. Why should she have a whole day to enjoy herself?

Other women did, though. But they had a servant man that they could leave the hens and the milking to. James would never agree to their having a man in to help. He said he couldn't see the sense of it; why would they both be away from house at the same time? Still, when it came to a question of who should go, Eleanor always stayed behind. Maybe it was her own fault; she

15

should be firmer and not give in so easily. But she never was able to ask James for anything without nerving herself for hours beforehand. And each year it was getting harder and harder to talk to him at all.

By bedtime she was too tired to care anymore and she put out James's clean shirt and socks with a slight feeling of relief that tomorrow she would be alone in the house. She wouldn't bother about a dinner; tea would do, and she could have it in comfort without his dour face on the other side of the table.

Next morning was fine and warm and there was a slight haze that promised a really hot day. James was very cheerful, though he looked rather uncomfortable in his woolen shirt and blue serge suit. At breakfast time he talked quite a lot—only scraps of sentences about the time he would have to be at the station and what time the train would be back at night. But for him it was a long conversation.

He picked up his cap and went toward the door and as he wheeled out his bicycle he called, "Well, I'm away, Eleanor, and don't work too hard if it's hot." She stood in the doorway holding the teapot that she was going to empty and laughed with surprise. He turned round and smiled and rode off down the lane.

Eleanor went back into the house, humming softly, and began to clear up the kitchen before churning. *Don't work too hard,* she laughed to herself. He had never said that to her before; in fact he never seemed to notice that she worked at all. Maybe this holiday would change him. He would see all the other farmers' wives there and he might tell her to go out more. He might see the clothes in the shopwindows and suggest that she should buy her clothes instead of bringing her rolls of gray and brown cloth from the market. But perhaps that was too much to hope for.

She took up the bucket to go down the lane for water. As she pumped she could feel the emptiness of the countryside with everyone away at the excursion. Of course women with young children would still be at home, but they would have too much to do to be on the road. She decided that she wouldn't go away from the house at all today. She didn't want people to see that she had been left behind, even though she was quite happy about it now.

At dinnertime she had tea and buttered toast and a boiled egg. She ate it slowly, savoring the luxury of not having to jump up and down to serve James. Maybe from this on she could get him to talk at mealtimes and then he wouldn't be finished so quickly. Tomorrow she would ask about the excursion. She might even manage to stretch it out for four or five days or even a week if she didn't ask too many questions at once. Then he would grow into the habit of talking to her about anything. After all, other men talked to their wives.

She decided to pull the gooseberries and make jam in the afternoon even though it was warm. She pulled the gooseberries, and as she sat topping and tailing them, she planned the questions she would ask to make James talk of the excursion. Tonight she wouldn't bother him about it. He would be home late anyway and she would ask him only was he tired and was it very hot in the train. Then she would give him his supper and it would be bedtime. But tomorrow they would talk about the train journey and the Customs men, and the next day about the streets of Dublin and the shops and where he had got his dinner. And there would still be the men whom he had been with and the fields he had passed by—all that to talk about. It would easily last for a week and even after that he might remember little details to tell her about if she was careful always to be interested.

Things were going to be much easier now, she could feel that.

The kitchen was very hot now, for she had built a good fire to boil up the jam quickly. She might as well bake while the fire was hot, though there were wells of perspiration at the hollows of her neck.

It was growing late as she laid the table for the supper, putting out the fresh bread and a pot of the new jam. Even if James didn't eat it, it would still look cheerful on the table. Maybe he might eat it now if he was hungry and then he might grow to like jam and she wouldn't have to watch it on her shelves covered with blue mold.

When everything was ready she sat down in the doorway to cool and wait for him to come home. The sun set and a breeze blew up and she began to worry about why he hadn't come back yet. The kettle had gone off the boil and she gathered up twigs and a few small pieces of coal to boil it up again. It was practically dark now, so she lit the lamp and sat down by the fire.

At last she heard footsteps in the lane and waited where she was, expectancy keeping her very still. He might even have brought her a present; he had been in such good form in the morning. Then she realized that there was somebody else with him. She could hear the footsteps of two or three men. That was strange, but cheering, for if James had a few more friends it would do him good. She stood up as the door opened and they came in. With a shock that made her feel sick she saw that James was drunk—so drunk that he had to be half-carried by the two neighbors that were with him. They put him down in the first chair they saw near the door. He slipped sideways but Eleanor didn't move from the fire with her hand on the back of the chair as she had risen.

Both the men wiped their foreheads and cleared their throats and then one of them said, "He'll be all right after a while, Mrs. Teggart. Don't worry about him. We were all hot after the train when we got to Dublin and we went into a pub opposite the station in Amiens Street. The rest of us went out after a drink or two, but he stayed on. Some of the men looked in before the train in the evening and the barman said he had been there all the time. He's not used to drink—that's why he's so far gone."

Eleanor thanked them coldly and politely, though her lips were so stiff that each word was an effort. The men slipped out, closing the door after them.

She sat down slowly, without taking her eyes off him as he slumped with his mouth open and one leg stuck straight out in front of him. She could do nothing for him; she couldn't go near him although she knew he ought to be helped to bed. Then he got up suddenly and began to lurch about the kitchen.

As she watched him her numbness gave place to violent choking rage. He hadn't seen Dublin at all. He had sat drinking in one public house opposite the station for hours, seeing nothing, hearing nothing. There would be no conversation to be made out of that. What right had he to take the day and waste it when she could have made such good use of it? He staggered toward the fireplace, groping blindly for the mantelpiece. She watched him, tight-lipped, and then a wild urge made her push him furiously in front of the fire. He threw up his hand, grabbing at the mantelpiece as he fell, and pulled himself into the chair.

Her legs felt weak and she sat down slowly, one hand on her cheek and the other holding the table. She couldn't look at him anymore. What had possessed her to try and push him into the fire? That was murder—she

19

might have killed him. That was what she had come to—
murder. Or maybe she had imagined it all.

She turned round quickly and looked at him. He was
half-lying in the chair with his eyes open, staring at the
ceiling. His cap was lying at the side of the fire. It was
scorching slightly. It made her head swim as she smelled
it. She got up and went slowly to bed, holding on to
every article of furniture as she passed it.

Theresa

During the last year of the war, Theresa was so reck-
lessly gay that some of the neighbors began to whisper
gossip about her. "I know it's jealousy that's wrong with
them," her mother said. "But I hate you to give them the
chance to say things about you. You shouldn't be going
out with American soldiers at all," she scolded when
Theresa came in even later than usual. "You know quite
well they get a girl a bad name."

Theresa laughed. "They get a girl lovely presents,"
she said and she reached up to stroke her mother's
cheeks with the new fur gloves she was wearing. "Aren't
they nice and soft? My hands won't ever be cold again,"
and she pressed them against her own face.

Her mother had to smile at her. "All the same,

Theresa, this won't last," she said. "What I've always wanted is for you to marry some nice man who'll be good to you. It's not like when I was married and bringing you all up; the men have work now."

Theresa interrupted her. "Ah sure, that won't last either," she scoffed and banged out of the room.

One morning she told her mother that she was going to have a baby. Her mother sat down and cried. Theresa turned her back so that she wouldn't have to look at the way her mother's face had crumpled. "I'm not the only one," she said sulkily. "There's plenty of other girls worse than me." Her mother didn't answer her and she shouted, "Oh, don't go on like that. What good will that do? I'll have the baby in the hospital and I'll leave it in the home and I'll be back at work the same as I always was."

But it didn't happen like that. She didn't ask to see the baby when she woke after the birth; she closed her eyes again after one glance round the ward. She'd had a bad dream, she told herself, and she wasn't right awake yet. If she opened her eyes in a minute she would find herself at home. Then she saw a young fair-haired nurse carrying the bundle. Theresa kept her eyes on the nurse's face and thought how nice she looked and wished her hair would turn out that color when she put bleach on it. The nurse laid the baby in the crook of Theresa's arm, and Theresa gasped as she looked into the screwed-up black face with the flattened nose and thick lips. This wasn't hers, she thought, pushing it away. The baby whimpered and the nurse bent over her. "Hold it like this." She showed her. Theresa lay there, staring straight ahead, until the weight on her arm became uncomfortable. Then she put her other arm round to ease it, and for a moment the baby was pressed warmly against her

breast. Suddenly she tightened her arms so that the baby was turned toward herself. She rubbed her cheek against the blanketed head and then looked round aggressively. Nobody was looking near her, though, and when the nurse came to take the baby away all she said was "I forgot to tell you it's a girl."

Afterward, when she should have been resting, she began to worry. She was puzzled about the whole business; he hadn't been black. Not that it mattered now— the baby had to be looked after whether it was black or not. But how could she manage to keep the child safe from people who would jeer at her for being a nigger? Presently a nurse, seeing her awake, gave her a tablet to make her sleep.

In the morning she smiled when she got the baby in her arms again. She felt the fuzz of black hair with the tip of her finger. *She'll have curly hair*, she thought. *And she is nice-looking—far nicer than a whole lot of those skinny red babies.* But the black skin showed up very darkly against the white shawl she was wrapped in.

"I'm bringing her out to have her baptized," the nurse said. "What name do you want for her?"

Theresa had never considered a name and no name would come into her mind, so she asked, "What's your name, nurse?" and the nurse laughed.

"Deirdre," she said. "My mother was romantic!"

It was an unusual name, Theresa thought, and smiled at the nurse. "Yes, I'd like that. She might as well have a nice name at least."

In an hour's time the baby was brought back to her. "There you are," the nurse said. "Nothing left but Christians, children of God and heirs to the kingdom of heaven. She has great lungs too; you should have heard her shouting when the water was poured on!" Theresa

23

laughed with pride and then lay looking into the baby's face, admiring the long black eyelashes that were unnoticeable against the dark skin. She slept then, but started the moment the nurse tried to lift the baby away from her, and didn't yield until she was fully awake.

All the time she was thinking how she was going to look after the baby when she left the hospital. She'd have to be watching all the time for fear anyone would harm the child. It wouldn't be so bad until she began to walk; she'd be able to keep her safe. She'd have to stay off work, but the munition factories were all closed since the war had ended anyway, and she had never done any other work.

It wasn't till her mother came to see her that she was reminded of her original plan. She hadn't had time to think of her mother until she saw her at the door of the ward. Her mother's determinedly cheerful expression gave her a sense of relief; she would have someone to help her care for the baby. Her mother hurried up to the bed and then saw the black skin of her granddaughter. "My God!" she whispered, staring at the baby's face. Then she looked at Theresa. "Are they good to you?"

Theresa felt sick at the sight of her mother's anxiety; she assured her that everybody was very kind to her.

"How about the nuns?"

"The nuns?" Theresa echoed wonderingly.

"Will the nuns take it into the home when it's black?" her mother asked and it came back to Theresa that she had meant to put the baby into the home. But she couldn't leave Deirdre in the home. Deirdre was hers. Nobody else could mind her right.

"Do you hear me?" her mother asked, her voice sharpening, and Theresa answered defiantly, "They don't take black babies in the home."

24

Her mother cried out in alarm, "They've got to take it, d'you hear me? You've got to put it somewhere. I'm not going to have the people sneering at you for bringing home some nigger's brat!" Theresa was frightened. Her mother hated the baby, she could see. What would she do if the baby wouldn't be safe from malice in her own home?

Her mother sat in silence for a while. Then she got up and stooped over the bed to press Theresa's arm that was round the baby. Theresa was dimly aware of the warm firm touch even after her mother's quick footsteps had left the ward.

But when the nurse was settling her for the night she asked, "What are the nuns like? I mean, are they good to the children?" and listened to the nurse's assurance that the nuns were careful and kind. By morning she had made up her mind that Deirdre would be safer in the home, and she asked the nurse to send word to the nuns and then refused to think of it anymore until her mother came to see her again. The lines on her mother's face seemed deeper, she thought.

"Theresa," she began, "would you like to bring the baby home with you?" Theresa shook her head. "You can bring it home with you if you like, now," her mother continued. "Your father and I won't let anybody say a word against you."

Theresa shook her head again. "I know that," she said. "But you don't like the baby."

"Well—" her mother said hesitantly and then tried to explain. "You see, it's only that you'd never rise up again if you have the child with you always, but if it's what you want—"

"You don't like her," Theresa interrupted. "I'm send-

ing her to the nuns," and her mother's face showed her relief.

"It's just as well, maybe," she said wearily. "Your father was paid off on Friday."

Theresa looked at her in dismay. Then she consoled her mother. "I'll be able to work all right. At any rate, you're not to go out charring the way you used to before the war."

And after a couple of weeks at home, Theresa was glad to go out to work in one of the mills. The work tired her out, but it served to deaden the aching desire to have Deirdre with her. At odd moments of the day and night, though, the warm milky smell of the baby would haunt her, making her head swim with the fierceness of her longing. She caught several of her parents' anxious glances and tried to shake off her listlessness. "Would you not think of going to the pictures, love?" her mother asked three or four times and Theresa forced herself to smile.

"Yes. Maybe. Tomorrow, or the next night—or some night there's a good picture on."

At times her mother's brooding solicitude annoyed her. When she asked, "What sort of women are you working with?"

Theresa shrugged. "They're all right."

Her mother persevered: "Is it true that some of the men aren't respectful to you?"

"Ach, could you blame them!" Theresa flared and her mother was afraid to question her again. After a while people grew used to the change in her and didn't bother her anymore.

Then one Sunday, something happened that made it impossible for Theresa to leave the baby in the home any longer. The new parish priest made the announcements

and then asked them please to listen as he had something important to say. There was a rustle of interest, but Theresa didn't stop fiddling with her prayerbook. The priest began, "I believe that there are girls in this parish who had children during the war, and that they put them into the orphanage." Theresa kept her head bent, but she could see her mother's hands clenched round her beads. "Those children," the priest continued, "were brought into the world without any hope of a father's protection and care. That's over and done with, but is it any reason for denying those same children a mother's love? The nuns are good to them, but how can they give a couple of hundred children the same attention that you can give to one or two? Supposing, even, that they're quite happy in the orphanage, what happens when they are fourteen? They're sent to work with tradesmen or as servants. Some of them will find good homes, but how can you be sure that your child won't fall into the hands of someone who wants only cheap labor?" Theresa was staring at him. This was Deirdre he was talking about. Deirdre mightn't be happy in the home—that's what he was saying. She could hear only scraps of what followed. "I know it's hard for all of you, impossible for some. . . ." Theresa thought frantically, *I've got to do something. I can't leave her there,* and she heard nothing except the end of what the priest said: "And if any girl is brave enough to bring home her child, she needn't be afraid of what people will say. I will publicly disgrace any person who says a word against her." The people, subdued, slid to their knees and only Theresa remained sitting.

She'd have to bring Deirdre out of the orphanage— there was no doubt about that. But where in the name of God was she going to bring her? She wasn't going to leave her at home with her mother and father when they

bore the child such a grudge. She would have to get married. . . . There was Harry Mulholland; he used to ask her every other week to marry him. But that was before Deirdre was born. Nevertheless, she would ask him in the evening. . . .

When she was preparing to go to his house she felt angry with herself for having become so drab looking. Her clothes had worn shabby and all the blond part of her hair had grown out. She tried smiling at herself in the mirror but her face seemed all dragged down. *Dear knows he'll not like me much the way I've got,* she thought. But she could try anyway.

Harry looked startled when he opened the door and then he burst out laughing at her. He pointed to the rocking chair in the corner and Theresa sat down and looked round the untidy kitchen without speaking. At least she could make the house more comfortable for him, and Deirdre could be very happy in it. Then she turned to Harry, sitting rubbing his hands in embarrassment.

"Would you like to marry me now?" she said.

Harry's eyes widened and then he laughed uneasily. Theresa, watching him, saw all the things that had made her consistently refuse to marry him before: the way his nose curved down over his upper lip and the little tuft of hair that he couldn't get at with his razor because of it, and the big soft grayish-colored ears he had. He was bending one over with his fingers, and flaking off chapped skin from the top of it. She wondered now at her silliness in even attaching any importance to such things. "You used to want to marry me," she prompted him.

He cleared his throat. "Well, you see. . . ," he began, and then licked his lips. "Well, dammit, Theresa, you used to be full of fun and laughing every time I'd see you. That was why I wanted you. If I thought," he said

then, "if I thought that you'd forget about what's happened and be the same again, I'd marry you in a flash." He glanced at her hopefully but Theresa looked away from him into the fire. "You see, I want to have Deirdre with me," she said.

Abstractedly she watched the flames weld the black coals into a glowing shape. Then Harry put back his head and shouted with laughter, and slapped his thigh and rocked backward and forward. "By heavens, that'd give the street something to talk about!" he laughed. Theresa smiled dutifully; it felt a rather stretched smile. "You and me and what do you call her? Deirdre? A ready-made family! I can just hear ol' Mrs. Munro and the Skillens talking about it, and what my poor mother, God rest her, would have said," he continued chuckling.

"But they're not allowed to talk about it," Theresa told him, and when she had explained, he began to laugh again.

"That's rich," he roared and then he turned to her excitedly. "We'll do it," he said. "We'll get married and you go for the child and we'll wheel it out for all the ol' crones to look at, and if they as much as turn their heads we'll threaten the priest on them. Didn't I think all the fun had ended with the war. But we'll get a lot of crack out of this yet!"

Theresa smiled and got up to go. She would have liked him to settle all the details at once but she was too tired to stay any longer. She was a bit disconcerted by his bursts of laughter; she wasn't sure that it would be good for Deirdre to be treated as a huge joke, but she would have a home in which to rear her and that was the main thing.

When they returned from the weekend's honeymoon in Dublin, Theresa went to fetch Deirdre from the nuns.

They congratulated her and praised her and said what a fine baby Deirdre was, until Theresa's heart warmed and she started back home without the feeling of apprehension that had been with her since her marriage. Deirdre was well wrapped up so that very little of her could be seen, but when they came near home she began to cry and fight until she had her arms free of the tightly wound shawl. Then she waved her fists in the air and crowed, till the children playing in the street shouted their delight in "the lovely wee brown baby."

Many a time Theresa was glad that she was able to trust them to wheel Deirdre out in the big cream-colored pram that Harry bought for her. She had to get Deirdre out of sight if she wanted peace from Harry's great gusts of laughter. For Harry the joke never seemed to pall. Every fine Saturday and Sunday he insisted on Theresa and himself wheeling the big pram through the poor streets and up into the suburbs of prim villas, and he shouted laughter into the startled faces of other strolling couples. When Deirdre grew a little older she laughed too and cheered and banged the pink rattle Harry had given her against the side of the pram. To keep up the pretense of enjoyment Theresa had to smile too, but there were nights when she was so tired that she wanted never to see Harry or Deirdre again. She kept telling herself that she enjoyed having Deirdre with her, but she was such a big boisterous child, and she always made Theresa feel so ashamed with Harry. By the time she was two, Theresa had the first of Harry's children to look after as well. Theresa thought that the new baby would take his mind off Deirdre, but he seemed to look on his son only as a foil for Deirdre's darkness. She chased Deirdre out to play as much as possible, and she was grateful to the neighbors for being so good to her. The

children didn't fight with Deirdre either because she was so big and strong and dictatorial.

Still, when she was five and had to go to school Theresa began to wonder if the strange children's parents would object to her being there or if the teachers would refuse to take her in. She mentioned it to Harry one evening but he wouldn't take it seriously. "Aha, so she's going to school is she?" he laughed at Deirdre. "You'll knock 'em cold!" And he began sparring with her, shouting, "Come on, Joe Louis!" and Deirdre yelled and flailed the air with her dark brown fists, and their three other children banged and shouted too. Theresa, in the rocking chair, was worn out trying to prevent the youngest from bouncing off her knee in his excitement. When the noise had subsided, except for one of the children howling on the floor because Deirdre had bumped into him and knocked him down, Harry said, "Do you know, I believe I'll take the day off tomorrow and bring her down to school myself."

Theresa protested immediately. "Oh, no, no, I can't let you do that. I'll have to do it." Harry turned away from her and cuffed the child who was howling, but in the morning he went off to work as usual and left Theresa to bring Deirdre to school.

Walking down the street, holding her tightly by the waist, Theresa thought Deirdre didn't look too bad. When she was well scrubbed she looked like somebody out of the pictures. Theresa kept on giving her directions as to how she was to behave, until the baby-room door opened after her hesitant tap, and a fat round-faced young teacher came out. Theresa wished she didn't look quite so young; she didn't like having to explain about Deirdre to anyone who appeared so childish.

But the teacher, without seeming the least surprised,

told Deirdre to go in and find a seat for herself. Theresa bent forward to give the child an encouraging shove, but Deirdre marched straight up to the front seat, pulled a little girl off it and sat down herself, surveying the room belligerently. Theresa and the teacher watched her and Theresa, shamefaced, said, "I'm afraid she'll be a bother to you. The father has her ruined." At that the teacher raised her eyebrows and Theresa hastily explained, "My husband, I mean," but the teacher was in a hurry to get back into her room to quell the uproar that had arisen.

She waited only to tell Theresa, "Be sure and keep her at school every day. She'll be making her first Holy Communion soon."

Theresa walked home slowly, wondering how Deirdre was ever going to get through such an ordeal as that would be. She would be dressed in a white frock and veil that would make her blacker than ever and she would have to walk down the aisle facing a packed church. As the months passed and the date fixed for it came nearer, Theresa had moments of complete panic. Tentatively she suggested asking the teacher if she would arrange that Deirdre should make her first Holy Communion quietly by herself at an earlier Mass. Harry objected that it wouldn't be fair to Deirdre. "Once you begin that, God knows where it would end," he said and Deirdre, who was listening began to bawl, "I want a white dress, so I do! I want a white dress!" The other children joined in with her crying and for the sake of peace Theresa gave in.

During the early part of the Mass, Theresa knelt with her head bowed, too afraid even to watch what Deirdre was doing. Gradually the comfort of Harry's burly presence encouraged her to look up, and she saw that the teacher had brought Deirdre to the end of the seat beside

her. She was pleased, and surprised when, watching
Deirdre walk back from the altar with her hands joined
demurely and her tight little black eyes roving round the
church, she heard several women murmur, "Ah, God
love it, will you look!" Theresa sat up in the seat, feeling
weak, suddenly. She listened with absorbed attention to
the curate who began his talk by asking the children
which they would rather have—a good long sermon or a
big cup of tea and a fry. Theresa smiled when she heard
Deirdre's voice loud over the rest, shouting for "a fry."
He had always been nice to Deirdre.

When she came out he was standing at the top of
the steps, talking to a bunch of children. Deirdre pulled
away from her and ran over to the group. The other
children stood back to let her pass and she walked
straight up to the priest. "Father, bless my beads," she
said peremptorily, holding up a pair of red beads Harry
had given her.

"Ah, it's Deirdre herself," Father Harvey said heartily. "How are you at all? Man, but you're great style.
Stand out there till I see you." Theresa, watching Deirdre
preen herself, thought how cold and lifeless and anemic
the other children looked beside Deirdre's healthy over-
flowing vigor. Then she heard Harry's laugh from the
crowd of men at the foot of the steps and, hurrying forward with Deirdre's coat, Theresa took her home.

Harry came home in great form shortly afterward,
and when breakfast was over he suggested taking
Deirdre out of Theresa's way for a while. "I'll bring her
downtown and get her photograph taken," he said.

"You'll do no such thing," Theresa said, appalled.
"You'd have everybody laughing at her."

But Harry persisted. "She'd enjoy it, you know. I'm
all for letting her have what fun she can get now."

Theresa repeated that Deirdre wasn't going and, calling her in from the street where she was playing, began stripping off her white dress and veil. She was aware of Harry watching her and she was irritable with the child. She smoothed the long folds of white satin clumsily, conscious of her haggard face and of her body swollen with pregnancy. Then she asked crossly, "What's wrong with you? What are you staring at me for?"

He came over and fingered the stuff of the frock. "Do you remember you had on a white shiny thing like that the first time I asked you to marry me?" Then he put his hands on her arms. "Look, go on downtown now and buy a new dress just like it," he said eagerly.

"Sure, I would only look daft," Theresa protested, half-angrily.

"You wouldn't look daft, you'd look grand," he coaxed her. "Go on now. Your mother and father will be over this evening. Why don't you dress up and have a good time for once and let me see you laughing again."

Theresa's eyes lighted for a minute and then she rejected the idea: "I can't have a good time when I have Deirdre on my mind," and when he tried to sweep that away she insisted: "Harry, what's going to happen to her when she grows up? How's she going to get married? How's she going to get work? What in the name of God is she going to do? And I can't do anything for her. I can't even think of it. I can't face it at all—"

"Hey, hey, hey, hold on," Harry interrupted her, laughing. "Did I hear you say 'can't'? Did I? Harry Mulholland doesn't know the meaning of the word 'can't.' Amn't I in with you on this? Of course you'll see her through. You'll be able to help her all right, won't you? You'll feel better about it when you're not so tired. Come on now, won't you?"

And to please him she said, "Maybe," but her voice was still wavering. She noticed the way she was clenching the white frock and she sat down with it over her knee, stroking it. She watched her hands till they stopped trembling, and then: "Yes, Harry," she said slowly. "Yes. Maybe I will."

The Pursuit
of Happiness

"Remember, Josephine, I want you to be happy."

Stout Aunt Sybil settled her gray hair smoothly over the top of her head and, bolstered by the importance of her ponderous bust, pouter-pigeon-wise surveyed her niece.

"Oh well, I am," Josephine answered, wishing there were a safe secret place where one could hide happiness and save it from sour-grape fingers that raked it and tossed it aside in the way of penniless women in a bargain basement. She sought refuge behind her tea tray, dispensing hospitality with slow placid movements.

"I know, dear, you are very loyal to your father and brother, but you can tell *me* the truth. It's foolish to pretend. I saw you downtown one day last week and, my

37

dear, your face! People were turning to look at you, you were so depressed. And I assure you it did not improve your looks; you were positively ugly."

Josephine shrugged off her annoyance. "We all have our off days," she retorted, refusing to recall anytime last week.

"I tell you I never saw you look so down. You were coming out of the city hall. It was Friday, I think. Yes, that's right—Friday. I didn't dare go near you at the time, but I made up my mind that I should come round and seriously speak to you on the matter."

Aunt Sybil's plump, well-cared-for fingers consciously caressed the stiff, silken sleeve of her coat.

"I am happy today. Will that do?" Josephine asked.

Her aunt smiled condescendingly. "It will not and you know it. You cannot stay here wasting your life any longer. Your father and brother can employ some woman to cook and clean for them. We are going to arrange this now. Happiness has to be worked for."

Her determination always aroused apprehension in Josephine and for a moment's respite she asked, "What *is* happiness?"

Her aunt forbade passage to the question with a hand always ready for point duty. "Now don't be cynical, Josephine, it doesn't suit you."

Josephine shook her head, sensible enough not to protest aloud. *My happiness is here one day, gone the next,* she thought. *Are there people for whom it is a constant state?* But she could not believe that. This morning, for instance, in the sour sparse soil under the dining room window, lily of the valley was rich with a broad, generous leaf and firm stalks bearing little hard green balls that would grow into delicate bells. She walked to Mass the long way over the brow of the hill so that she could catch

a glimpse of the lough with the black slope on one side and misty, wooded hills on the other. There was a silver track of bright glare down the center. In the crisp chill she crossed the road amid hurrying dungareed workmen to where the sun shone warm.

It shone on the window of a butcher's shop and the crystals of ice in frozen beef melted and a pool of blood lay on the white tiles. A thin old workman was standing outside, and catching Josephine's eye, he beckoned her over. "Look at that!" he said, pointing with excitement. "All the good running out of it. Wasted. Some poor beast killed in South America and its blood running out on a street in Belfast. Such waste! It's a wonderful world, eh? But I wouldn't touch a mouthful of that stuff. Would you?" And he raised his eyes to heaven, seeking agreement from the Almighty as well that His good world was being misgoverned.

This early-morning shower of gifts made her prayers soar full of gratitude. "We praise You. We bless You. We adore You. We glorify You." She had wanted it sung with organs playing and bells ringing. Still her happiness existed independently. It tingled the nerves under her skin, making her cheeks pink and her eyes dark and her movements light. In odd moments, though, there would come a silent tension as if she were uplifted by a daring hand and might be dropped any second. So that it was almost a relief when a day occurred that she was heavily earth borne and the tightrope was far out of her reach.

"You know, Josephine, dreamers never get any-where," Aunt Sybil ruled and Josephine laughed.

"How do you know I wasn't seeing visions?"

"Josephine, dear! You a visionary! Don't let's be fool-ish. I am not going home until you have definitely de-

cided what to do about this. What kind of a job would you like?"

"Well, I'm always threatening Father and Michael that I'll put one of those advertisements in the paper—'Settled Christian girl wants post for general service. Anything considered.' Or I could call myself a capable general, only its sound is domineering and I don't think I could live up to it."

Aunt Sybil disregarded this.

"I was thinking of one of those oil places in the Middle East for you. Mark Campbell is home at the moment from Abadan out there. There's a lot of trouble now, but I'm sure it will all blow over. His mother told me there are very, very few girls there and the men are all anxious to marry. You could have your pick."

Josephine made a gesture of distaste and her aunt leaned forward, tender consideration deliberately softening her voice.

"Now you really *will* have to admit that you want to be married. And you can't marry Peter, so it's no good being bitter about him any longer."

"Bitter about Peter? Ah, no."

But Aunt Sybil trampled on, undefeated. "It's only natural that you should feel badly treated."

The lambent brown eyes bent on Josephine in such concern irritated her. "Is it not possible to be now and again on a higher plane than what is merely natural?" she asked, and then, aware that she had sounded smug, she could no longer prevent her anger taking over. "Against whom should I bear a grudge? Against Peter for being ill? Against my father for obstructing my marriage when he was told he had a shadow on his lung and I thought I might have been able to cure him? Would that have pleased you? I'd be here, living this exact same life

I'm living now, but I would have a wedding ring on my finger. What benefit would that bring? You wouldn't have to explain and excuse my wasted life; everybody would know and pity me. Is that it? And I hate pity. It's slimy and cold and lifeless like the white turned-up belly of a black slug."

"Josephine!" Aunt Sybil gasped, round red spots on her olive cheeks. "And you said you were not bitter. A little bit jealous too, I think. My dear, a ring would bring you more than that."

"It would bring me the right to mourn in decency," Josephine said sadly, and then she smiled. "But it would bring me the compulsion to mourn and I would not mope to please any convention. The neighbors would say I was hard and unfeeling. As it is, they know and you know he has cast me off and wants no more of me. Therefore their huge glee lets me do as I wish."

"That is uncharitable and untrue," Aunt Sybil condemned her.

"It *is* true, but perhaps I should not have put it in words, They are very nice to me now. 'Poor Josephine' they call me and present me with little bouquets of heartsease over the hedge."

"Oh, aren't they really kind," Aunt Sybil said.

"When Peter had his health and I had his love, they were not so kind. They nagged my conscience interminably with wondering aloud how my father and Michael would manage when I married, and if my mother would have approved of my leaving them alone."

She remembered the day the previous spring, when among a carpet of bluebells on the hill Peter had found a white one. He had laughed with delight showing it to her and she touched the feathery curl at the end of a green-veined petal before he threaded it through his buttonhole

41

with solemn concentration. His hands were brown and strong and clumsy. It was that day first that Josephine's fingers combing his wiry hair felt the pricks of perspiration on the hot skin and wondered why she should be cold. Her lips would produce no false smile to greet Mrs. Bates, who bared plastic teeth to shout, "It's great to be young and happy no matter who comes to the wall." It would have been easy to believe medievally in the evil eyes they had put on them, these envious women, to blame them for the rot that set in in his lungs and took his body from her, and the peevish irritation that built a barrier Everest-high round him, blocking her out.

"You should go over more often to see his mother. It is even harder for her than for you," Aunt Sybil prompted.

"I don't really think she wants me. She is heartbroken but she resents my intrusion; she wants to suffer in luxurious privacy. 'What can you know of grief with your little petty self-love?' she said to me. 'You have never had a son and watched him wearing away.' 'And is not that a grief,' I asked her, 'that I shall have no son now?' But she didn't heed me."

"But you said you did not mind about him anymore and were quite happy, Josephine." Aunt Sybil sighed. "I don't know where I am with you at all."

"Neither do I," Josephine answered, and then a brilliant bar of sunlight isolated her from the shaded room and like an animal picked out by a car's headlamp she crouched forward in pain, all her courage ebbed; it was the same anguish that had leaped at her one wet night in the winter when she had gone to post Peter a letter.

The mizzle had drifted like a blue-green veil under the light of the big lamp at the corner and the little drops on the mouth of the pillar-box slid on her letter, smearing

his name. It was spotting his pillow beside the open window in the sanatorium, making him shake with cold; his bed creaked sometimes with his shivering. This she thought with sweet sadness, seeing herself as a resigned figure bent under the trials of a hard world and a loving God. And the derision became suddenly desolation and she put out her hand to steady herself on the pillar-box before she could walk home through the thick damp air.

Aunt Sybil embraced her, her cheek cool and soft, smothering her in the perfume of middle-aged self-satisfaction. Josephine had often wondered if all these women used perhaps the same soap or powder, or was it just the scent of a placid padding of flesh that had ceased to be a racked irritation? "Don't worry, Josephine, my dear. Just leave everything to me. I'll see you are settled with something good. I'll arrange everything." She sailed out, pausing at the door to assure Josephine that she'd be back soon, very soon.

"No peace on earth." Josephine raged impotently against the state Aunt Sybil had left her in. She cleared away the tea things noisily, hoping vaguely to eradicate her presence from the room. "She's an overwhelmingly kind woman," her father always said with measured charity, and the certain truth in that made Josephine feel guilty during her spells of hatred for her aunt's unimaginative impertinence. *If she goes near Peter or his mother and talks about me I'll not bear it*, she thought, bathed in humiliation, and started to the telephone to ring her and order her not to.

She stopped then. What did it matter? The Friday her aunt had seen her leaving the city hall she had been paying the rates to a fine, big gray-haired man. For something to say as she folded his receipt he told her that it was thirty years since he had taken over that stool and

43

that section of the counter. Watching the strong, cheerful face she had a great need to know how to cope with day after day of living. It had seemed to her then, and again now as her hand grew cold on the phone, that she had stepped outside of life. It was as if she stood near the edge of a dark lake watching ripple follow ripple endlessly while the sun rose and warmed and set without affecting them any more than they affected her. Dread drained her, leaving first her head and then her body empty, so that she was nothing but a taut skin and a dizzy fear that was—but was not felt. She could bear pain, it brought at its height an instant's satisfaction; but this emptiness she could not bear. She covered her face with her hands in order to feel skin on skin, but the consciousness of her posture made her scoff at herself.

Her father came in, immersed himself in his paper before dinner, and fell asleep in his armchair after dinner. But Michael exclaimed, "Aha! So Madame has been here. What's she up to this time? Does she still want to press you into the women's air force?"

"No. I'm to comfort some oil executive in the Iranian desert," Josephine laughed. Then she asked anxiously, "But how did you know?" With her father she knew she was safe from either perception or inquiry; provided his family were clothed and fed they could want for nothing. With Michael she was free from question, but he belonged to the same generation and she was always afraid of his interest.

"Did you not see these books she left you?" he asked. "It's a wonder she didn't mention them." Josephine felt a renewal of affection for her aunt; she knew what an effort it must have been for her to forgo parading her gifts. "You can put them safely in your bottom drawer until she comes back," Michael said. "You'll never read them.

Critical essays by some university lecturer, a travel book, and a biography of an actor! She'll never face the fact that she has a niece who reads only fiction." He yawned. "If the rain was eased I'd take the dog for a walk."

"Rain?" Josephine said, wondering, and then she remembered the exultation she had felt last night when it had been stormy and wet. The chimney smoke from brick houses splashed dark red, swooped down through the apple trees pink with the hope of blossom, and the blackened skeletons of the trees in the road showed through tenaciously tender new leaves.

She parted the curtains to look out. Immediately the light streaked out on the wet asphalt but the rain would not let it lie. Josephine watched dully for a long time as it was kept moving, jagging, shimmering, restless, unreflective. Then her attention was seized and concentrated until it seemed to her that she had mistaken the order of things. It was not that the rain disturbed the light but the light that tortured the rain. She had it then in the power of a jerk of her wrist to cut off the light, and in the dark the rain would slip easily, steadily, into the receptive earth. Besides, the slightly parted curtains looked untidy both from the road and from the room. On an impulse she whirled back the wine velvet with a clatter of rings so that the whole stretch of the road was laid open with the flashing blade of a curved sword. Sometime outside her power the rain would cease, and the light would rest in calm, broad, shining peace.

A Farm of Land

The entire countryside was horrified last week when the news leaked out that Susan Lavery had sold her father's farm. The men spat with disgust and lamented the way young people nowadays had no respect for the dead and their wives said they weren't surprised. "A kite-headed carried-away being she always was," they said, in spite of the fact that Susan is a settled married woman with her family growing up round her. But none of them really knew Susan or cared why she had rejected her inheritance.

Susan wasn't born in that farm, nor were her two brothers who died in the 1919 flu. They were reared down in the Moss where her father's and mother's people had lived since the time of the Plantations. I never

visited them there; they had moved up to the big farm before I was born. But I saw their house with its mud walls crumbling and the broken roof beams lying among the nettles, and the little swampy fields sloping down to the lough with somebody else's cattle standing knee-deep in water in them. It was a lovely place in spring when the lough was bright blue and all the long banks of whins blazoned gold. And in summer when the sun shone, the spirals of heat were trapped by the high hedges so that the blue butterflies and scarlet dragonflies were languid and hung motionless over the brown drains. Not that I ever heard Pat Lavery say a word about that. "Bah," he would shout. "Corn that light that the threshing would be over in an hour and haystacks no higher than my head."

If he was in good humor he would laugh at that, for he was very short and powerfully broad. He used to make me uncomfortable when I was about sixteen and very sensitive about my girth when he thumped me between the shoulder blades and bellowed, "You and me belong to the bulldog breed—eh? Short in the leg but right and thick in the chest!" And I had to pretend to enjoy the joke, for he was an old man and meant to be a kindly one. But if he was in a serious mood he could talk for hours about the poor land it was and the misery of farming it when the mists lay waist deep on it till dinner-time and the water oozed up between the tiles in the kitchen floor. His father had already saved a couple of hundred pounds toward buying a better farm and Pat went on from there. "I swore by Almighty God," he would say with the air of a prophet of the Old Law, "that neither me nor my children would spend the rest of our lives hunkering under a whin bush out of the rain. I swore I would get out of the bog and by God, I did."

I have heard Susan tell repeatedly how he managed it. He did all the buying and selling himself and it was only by the tone of his voice in the evenings that they knew whether he was satisfied or not. He provided rolls of cloth for the whole family, good hard-wearing gray or brown stuff that made suits for the boys and coats and dresses for Susan and her mother. Not one halfpenny of money did any of them ever see from one year's end to the next. Flour, tea, and sugar were brought home in the cart when he went into the market. One time, Susan gathered wild raspberries that grew along the Featherbed road and her mother begged Pat to bring home sugar to make jam since the fruit had cost nothing. He agreed, but when he found that with the extra bread that was eaten he had to buy another bag of flour, he laid down the law that not another pound of jam was to be made in his house.

Most of this, Susan laughed at; the raspberry incident she told as a joke, and she remembered her mother and herself giggling at the sight of her father arriving home late one night and the water dripping out of him after walking five miles across the bog to his cousin's house to get old schoolbooks so that he wouldn't have to give her a shilling to bring to school for them. Then she won a scholarship to the convent school and he wouldn't let her take it. It just didn't occur to him that she should take it. When she came home from school and told them about it he was delighted and praised her and told her what a grand girl she was, and that he was proud of her. The following morning he told her to ask the teacher to write to the nuns for him, to tell them she couldn't take it. When she protested he brushed her aside impatiently. "My God, girl, where do you think the money would come from for your bus and your clothes and your

books? We'd never leave the Moss if I spent money on trifles like that."

So Susan stayed at school till she was fourteen and then was sent to work in a fruit shop in Lurgan. The teacher had suggested that she should go as a maid to one of the big farms so that she shouldn't have to cycle to and from Lurgan every day. But Pat swore no daughter of his should be a servant in another man's house. This I heard from the countrywomen's gossip, not from Susan. Susan never mentioned that time at all. She was about eighteen and her brothers were a few years younger than she, when they both died of the flu. But she continued to work for the next four years until one day when she saw her father standing out on the frozen road watching for her coming.

She was surprised, she said, and even more surprised when he took her by the arm and helped her off the bicycle. "You're cold and tired, I know Susan, but come in," he said. "I have news will warm the cockles of your heart. Aye, and you're not going back to work either, so you'll not be tired any longer." I have heard Susan describe the evening over and over again, to me, to my mother and to her own children and always with the same glow of pride. The kitchen was bright when she went in, with a piled-up turf fire and the lamp's squat orange flame, and her mother smiling at her. He led Susan up to the table and sat her down beside her mother. He clinked two bags on the table and then leaned over toward Susan. "I've told Agnes and now I'll tell you. I've bought the farm, Susan! I bought it today, but I haven't paid the money yet. I'm to bring it tomorrow," and he emptied the bags of notes and coins with a flourish so that some of the coins rolled and lay, burnished, on the floor. He laughed like a boy and lifted

them, spinning them up in the lamplight and slapping them down again with the rest of the money. He counted it all, while they watched and snapped rubber bands round the bundles of notes and built golden columns of money. When he had finished he piled it all back into the bags again and asked, "Well, Susan, hasn't it been worth it? Tomorrow we'll have our farm of grand rich land, and remember, Susan, it'll be yours in time too. Hasn't it been worth it?" he repeated and for the moment Susan says she forgot all that had been sacrificed.

But even after they moved up to their fine new farm, there was neither time nor money to spare. Money was needed to stock it and to build outhouses, so that there never was any to buy the furniture that would have made the long slated farmhouse a comfortable home. Their few sticks from the Moss looked small and poor in the new big kitchen and there was nothing but three iron bedsteads for the high-ceilinged bedrooms. Later on Pat began buying solid old-fashioned articles at auctions and when I knew the house it was well furnished, but that was after Susan left.

When Susan found that she was expected to help her father with the outside work on the farm, she refused. She would milk and churn and do housework but she would do no work in the fields. So her mother left her to look after the house and she went out to help Pat. I re-member her myself as an old woman in the pea field in July and in the sprout field in December trotting behind her husband like some patient bondwoman with the rain dripping out of the sack over her head. That left Susan sitting idle for long hours in the house while her mother and father were working, for there was no furniture to clean and except for baking bread and boiling potatoes there was little cooking to do. It must have been about

this time that Susan began her pretense of knowing nothing about farming. She keeps it up still; they laugh at her for it in our house. "Indeed," she says, "I would hardly know the difference between a barley field and a wheat field. I never did any outside work, you know." It made the other women say that she was "just a bit above herself."

What finally drove her into the town was her father's arrangement that she should marry Thomas Martin, who owned the next farm. He was a small, broad-backed man with a hanging underlip and a bullying manner. He was afraid of ever showing any gentle feelings lest he should not be considered manly. When Susan protested that she didn't like him her father said, "Ach, you don't like him! What the hell does that matter? Doesn't the land lie into ours? Look at the grand farm your children will have." Susan insisted that he had never spoken a civil word to her since they had come to live there, but he threw up his hands to heaven. "Good God, what do the girls want these days? Isn't he a good Catholic? Hasn't he a grand farm? I don't know what more you'd want." And he gave her so little peace that she went into Belfast and worked there for three years until she married a commercial traveler with a little money, which he splashed sky high. When her father ordered her to break off the engagement and come to her senses she refused, declaring that she was sick to death of scraping and saving and she was going to live in comfort from then on.

The strange thing is that she doesn't. She is always patching and darning and cutting down big garments into smaller garments so that her family many a time look as if they were clad in bits and pieces. And I have seen her five children stand round the table while they said grace and then make a sudden dive to grab a slice of bread because there never was enough to satisfy them.

Perhaps that was one reason why they enjoyed visiting Pat and Agnes in the country. For by that time there was never anything like that in their house. In fact anytime I stayed with them there was an overpowering generosity with everything except actual money. It was almost impossible to empty a glass of milk; as soon as half of it was drunk, Agnes appeared and filled it up from a big jug covered all over with tiny cracks. And slice after slice of soda bread was pushed quietly onto everybody's plate. When the table was crowded with farls of bread and big slabs of butter Pat would come in from the yard kicking yelping dogs out of his way and, beaming, would bellow, "Glory be to God, Aggie, is there a black fast on here? Get some more butter out there—and bread too. These childher'll be hungry. And put more sugar in their tea. They like it sweet." It didn't matter to him whether we liked it or not. Aggie smilingly complied.

If he fed Susan's children, though, he also made them work. In the beginning it was fun for them, but when they tired of it and wanted to play he wouldn't let them; he expected them to stick at it like paid laborers. One day when Susan herself was there he kept the eldest boy working in the hay field till it was dark night. When they came in Susan demanded to know what he meant by it. "I've got to toughen them," he explained. "I don't want mollycoddles for grandsons."

"They're not yours to decide about," Susan flared at him, but he interrupted her.

"They may not have my name but they're my flesh and blood, and they've got to do me credit," he shouted. "And they're grand boys too," he added, "but soft—soft! They need hardening. They could no more do what I did at their age. Why, look at your own two brothers driving into Belfast in the cart one night a week and coming home the next night. Could your bucko do that?"

Mary Beckett

Susan answered very quietly. "No, he couldn't, and thank God he'll never have to. His father will never drive him out of the house in the pouring rain to come home dying of the flu the next night. Please God I'll not be burying my sons at sixteen years of age." There was a great silence in the kitchen. Then the old man sat down heavily on the sofa and began dragging off his boots. Agnes hadn't stopped stirring the porridge pot on the fire. Her pale blue eyes, which were always slightly smiling, didn't change at all.

I thought Susan mightn't come back after that, but it seemed to make little difference between them. Susan seemed a bit more distant every time she met her father but he, each time I saw him for the remaining four years of his life, was as hearty and tempestuous as ever. He hired a boy to help him with the work but that was the only change. Then one day when the warm sun filled the yard with the smell of manure and the perfume of lime blossom and fresh peas, one of the horses fell in its stable in some awkward way and three or four big strong young fellows who were there loading a lorry tried to lift it. Pat stood watching them for a while and when they couldn't manage it he said, "Stand back there, childher," and heaved the horse on its feet by himself. He went in then to the kitchen and sat down by the table, which was covered with hot baked bread. When Agnes came in with an armful of sticks for the fire, he was dead.

She took it very quietly at the time; she didn't even lose her smile until a week or two afterward. Then she began to have meaningless fits of anxiety. Finally they centered on the dinner. Pat had always insisted on having his dinner at twelve sharp. I had never heard Agnes say one word about it during his life. Now she began worrying about putting on the potatoes earlier and earlier

every day. And a couple of months after Pat's death she had to be watched during the night or she would have been up building a fire to boil them. She showed surprising bursts of bad temper when anyone tried to prevent her.

Susan stayed to look after her. Now and then she was impatient when she looked at the buckets of boiled potatoes that were going to waste. But other times she yearned toward her mother as she would toward a sick child, humoring her, reminding her of good days they had had while the two boys were alive and her mother was still young. Sometimes she was rewarded with an odd hiccupy little laugh. And her hands, which always I had seen lying acquiescent in her lap, would make quick darting movements as if she were going to clap them, when Susan repeated something funny that had happened to them. But she caught pneumonia one night last winter padding about in her bare feet, and died in less than a week.

On the day of the funeral Susan left the neighbors in the kitchen and went out. When I looked through the window she was walking with her youngest boy through the big plowed field that sloped up from the house. It was a bleak gray day, but the sun broke through for a moment and lit the lime tree on the breast of the rise so that every branch and twig glowed with springing life. Susan and her son started up toward it, the little boy staggering in his haste, but the sky clouded over again, and they turned back, their feet heavy with the rich dark earth with its patches of muddy snow and brown pools skimmed with ice. "Old Pat used to stamp round just like that," one of the men said, "shouting to anybody at all about his grand fields."

"Oh, she's eager now that it's hers, although she

never did a hand's turn about the place while he was alive," a woman retorted tartly and just as Susan came in another added, "You'd think decency would have kept her in till we'd gone." Susan looked round at them all, unsmiling, and, in that stiff, unbending way she had with people not her own, refilled their cups and plates. She went back to Belfast the next day and the place lay desolate.

Now it is sold. Ten thousand pounds she got for her father's beautiful farm. She showed me the check with a gesture of vague dissatisfaction. I don't know why, unless she was thinking of rustling bank notes and shining gold sovereigns.

Saints and Scholars

The two women sat on either side of the fire, the one old, the other young—both gray. The sour heartburn of resentment had aged them both. The older woman said, "You've been a great disappointment to me, Lena. I don't mind telling you I thought a lot of you once. The first day you stepped out of your father's car in the yard I thought what a fine capable girl you were and how safe Malachy would be in your keeping. 'If I die, I'll know that he's cared for,' I said to myself. But I should have known, for you laughed when you met him."

"How could I guess then the deadly sin that was. But it wasn't at him that I laughed; it was the way that you introduced him. 'Here's my dairy,' you said, 'and here's my byre, and here's my tractor, and riding on it, here's

my son. And his big dark eyes behind thick glass widened and blinked and widened again and he shook hands and mumbled, 'Pleased to meet you,' and went into the house to change in my honor. I could just as easily have cried, for surely he disappointed me after the warmth in the eyes of his mother."

"The only way to please me was through him. But the neighbors all warned me no good would come of a match arranged between parents now, when the custom's died out. But he and his father left all to me and what could I do? You weren't being forced into it either, unless by your own hard, grasping nature."

"Is it hard or grasping to want a husband and home and a family? What other way would I get them except by making much of the boys in the dance hall who were afraid of my education?"

"Malachy had more education than you."

"Why has it always been used as a millstone to tie around my neck—my half-dozen years at the convent? Because of it I was urged neither to marry nor to stay at home with my father and brother. Instead I was to go to the city and sit at a desk and write out accounts, and add numbers. I told my father I'd just as soon sit on a stone in the heart of the desert till the sun would soften my head. Then it held up my marriage until Malachy took himself off to the town to learn music and French because I knew a little of both."

"Many a one would be glad of a husband taking such trouble."

"It showed he resented my having merits at all that he thought competed with his. He wanted to know what marks I had got in exams years before. Even after my hasty subtraction, the jealous light in his eye didn't aid the growth of respect between us."

"You insulted his books the first day you met him."

"So, even then he complained to you! I said what a pity it was he had no books I could read since he had acquired no others beyond those he needed in school and in the training college. That was all."

"Why would he need any more after his uncle had left him the farm?"

"Why then did he send to the town for a copy of every book that was in our bookcase at home? Even *Little Women* and *What Katy Did*, because I had read them. He could have borrowed them or even kept them, God knows. But no, he had to do it in secret. Aren't they standing inside there behind glass doors and green curtains, tempting me to mock him every time I dust them? Does he not see how ludicrous it is—this pillar of his scholastic reputation? Do you know what came into my head that first day when I saw his pitiful collection of grammars and algebras and expurgated Shakespeare? I made a great joke to myself, for I thought in the face of his puffed-up pride in his learning, 'It went to his head, but it never got in.' I was ashamed of my lack of loyalty then, but now you can think what you like!"

"Oh, there never was decency in you."

"There was till he outraged it!"

"You're no fit wife for any man, let alone for my son. Did you never think to make any return for the home and the name that he gave you? Do you never remember you're the mother of his son?"

"His son! There's no drop's blood's resemblance between them, thank God. Peter's like my people, like my mother, God rest her."

"Have you no respect then for your husband?"

"I can feel no respect for my husband. Don't you see that it grieves me! Don't you see that in despising him

I'm despising myself for being his wife? I have built him up and bolstered him up and he keeps the edifice for the neighbors to see and crawls out to me for pity. Did you never think why I've read nothing but these magazines you complain of, since Peter was born? Did you never think I was sick looking at faces in them empty of all but their lipstick? Just because I discovered that Malachy tortured himself with scrambling after my reading, I confined myself to these so that he could feel his lofty supremacy. I have gone to all lengths to encourage his self-respect. And now you fear he might get wild notions from reading these stories. All right, I'll burn them and buy no more. Let him do what he likes; I'll help him no more. His wish is for me to treat him as I would a toddler seeking comfort after falling. You began it. You deserve to know how your rearing has prospered, and the half-grown boy of forty I have for a husband."

"I brought him up well. If he's changed for the worse it's your doing."

"Do you notice how we both deny him a will of his own? Your kind of love and my hate both annihilate."

"You can't say you hate him. You mustn't say that. It's a terrible sin."

"It is, and what's worse, a wife unloving, unloved, loses caste. He made me pity him and my pity grew rancid and turned into hate."

"You had no call to pity him."

"He asked for it from the day and hour of my marriage. He began to show off the gay dog he had been in the town. He told me my clothes were not smart; I should dress in dark grays and light browns like a girl he had met. I laughed and said I wasn't the type; I was too short and my hair was just brown. Then he agreed that this girl had been slender and tall and fair-haired and

that indeed I might be too dull. I was cross and said it wasn't the usual thing to tell a wife she's plain until after the honeymoon's over. Now would you not think it a pitiful thing to boast to a new wife of past conquests?"

"You must have made him think that you didn't admire the way he looked after you."

"Nor did I. The room he had booked was poor, with paper-thin walls so that he whispered whenever he wanted to talk, and the food was rough and badly cooked and served by a girl with a sty on her eye who said 'Now' when she put down each dish as if the meal was a triumph. But would he complain to them or let me point out that the milk was sour and sauce had stained the cloth some time before we came!"

"It was little enough to put up with."

"That I know now. But then I had hopes that marriage with Malachy might prove to be good and I dreaded to see the beginning spoiled. After the second day I cared no more."

"It does you no credit to remember and complain so long afterward."

"There never was anything good to blot out the memory of Malachy debasing himself to me by bemoaning the fact that this girl had laughed at him—this elegant girl whom I was to copy. And I had to reassure him every day that no girl could laugh in the face of his grand education, his hundred acres, and his thousands of pounds. I wanted to smother him, to strangle him, but instead I praised him when he gloated aloud over the way he had answered the girl when she refused to go to the pictures with him 'just in the way of friendship.' 'I have a girl of my own at home you know,' he said. That was me and still he appealed to me with glee in his voice, 'Wasn't I right? Lena, wasn't I right to show her I could get some-

body else?' Till the day I die I'll remember the loathing I felt."

"Why do you make me listen to this? After all, I am his mother."

"I couldn't tell anyone else, but you must hear my side to balance with his. He runs to you when I am more mocking than meek. But he doesn't even make any pretense of affection for me. He wasn't long back beside you and his barns and his beasts before the story had changed. 'If a man falls out with a girl, that's bad enough but it can always be mended,' he said one night when John Lavery and Eddie O'Rourke were in. 'But supposing to spite her he marries another. What then? His life is ruined; so's hers.' Then he leaned back and stuck out his stomach and sighed his melancholy for them both to condone. You should have seen the way their eyes darted from him to me. I airily said that I wouldn't imagine the wife would have a great time either, but it didn't put them off. You needn't pretend you didn't hear the story. But I can see it's now out of date. There's a better one now. First for money, then for spite. But the new one you and he have concocted makes my skin crawl. He married me for the sake of religion, for such was the will of God!"

"There's no need to sneer. And I don't know what disturbs you so much about that. I've always thought you were fairly devout. What are you so angry about?"

"I don't know, but it sickens me, disgusts and repels me. Malachy mouthing to God about me."

"You'll be sorry if you say any more."

"You're right, I suppose."

"I'm warning you, Lena, don't try him too far. These magazines have stories in them tempting men to leave their wives. They'd put ideas into his head when he's

hankering after this girl in the town. As he hinted to me, it's only his religion keeps him from going."

"Oh, I wish he would go and be done with it!"

"You said that before and I shouldn't be listening even. If he wishes for her it's your fault and the sin's on your soul."

"How nice for him. Let us say then that it is for the good of *my* soul that I wish he would go and find out this girl, if she even existed. But he won't. Think what would happen! It's eight years, you must remember. She's hardly plucking roses in the garden all these years waiting for him to return. Do you not imagine she'd laugh again at our poor Don Juan arriving to carry her off to Omeath, we'll say, or Blackrock; Dublin's too dear. She might even be more unkind than I am. He would have to face up to the fact that it's a clown he is and not a hero. It's much more comforting to be a martyr at home and respected as such, no matter what his mind is like. His thoughts don't let him down before the priest and parishioners."

"Lena, you're talking foolishness. He told me he wanted to marry the girl, but he was swayed by me and came home to you since you were trysted already. The girl hadn't a halfpenny."

"So the will of God was for him to marry money. All right. That offends me the least. But that isn't the whole, just the same. I was the easy way out. He needn't blame God when all he did was to take the line of least resistance."

"The Church says be advised by your parents."

"The Church says drunkenness is forbidden, still he gets drunk when he knows no one will see him. The Church says give to every man his own; still he boasts that he drives a hard bargain when he catches a man in a

corner. But when it says love your parents, he thinks he should hug himself into the shadow of your shawl till his bones are jelly and his blood flows anemic and thin."

"I needn't talk anymore. Your mind is made up that you won't accustom yourself to his ways. I'll go home. If it wasn't for my son and my grandson, I would trouble you little again."

"I have no quarrel with you. I would value your company."

"There's Peter now, swinging on the gate and stubbing his boots on the screenings. The roofs are wet. There must be a mist of rain.

"Peter, come in at once. You'll get wet. Let me see what your jersey is like. Dear goodness, it's soaking. Go and change. And your shoes. You'll have to change every stitch you have on and then I'll give you hot milk to keep you from catching a cold."

"You're fussing a lot, Lena, over a bit of a mizzle of rain."

"I dare not take any risk. I have no parents, no husband worth talking about. But no one on earth can deprive me of Peter. Remember, I too have a son." And her fingers dug in through wet wool and took hold of his bone and muscle.

The Balancing
of the Clouds

"In a hurry! Dear God," Charlotte jeered, "fifteen years to make up your mind and you in a hurry." Her voice rose hysterically and the bitch, startled, jumped up from her warm whinging pups and came over to Charlotte. John lunged his foot in its ribs and it squealed. Then the globe of the lamp cracked where the niggling tail of flame had worn it thin.

Alice Loughran, sleeping by the fire, gave a little spluttering moan and wakened. She rubbed her eyes with her fists and stretched langorously with a graceful relish in the heat. Looking round she shivered. "I must go home," she said and her voice was flat and her movements nervous and fumbling as she reached for her red corduroy hat, jaunty with a feather, and pulled it down

on her springing shaggy mop of auburn hair. She swathed her head, hat and all, in a black woolen shawl and stood up smiling at Charlotte with strong brave teeth and shy yellow heavy-lidded eyes.

"I'll put you a piece," Charlotte said, flinging her coat over her head and shoulders.

When she opened the door wood ash scattered over the teapot and the light wavered dull in the pools in the yard. By the stable a clump of Michaelmas daisies stood bedraggled, neglected. The gate clanged and the drops on the rail trembled and slid and dripped into the screenings thrown down in the gap. Rain shone black on naked branches in the orchard and mulched their withered leaves into the dark ground. The two shapeless figures bumped now and then, coggling uncaring over stones and in and out of muddy water. John Conlon shouldered the door to behind them.

"Did I say something wrong tonight?" Alice asked pathetically. "It's hard on other people when I say wrong things."

"You didn't say a word out of place," Charlotte assured her heartily, grieving that the lively excitable friend of her girlhood should have degenerated into this pitiable woman of fifty, a butt for giggles and guffaws. "You don't need to listen to John when he's cross. I'm always glad to see you."

"I wouldn't mind if he was cross with me," Alice said. "I don't listen when people are cross with me. But he shouted at you about you being old and we're not, and I said the first thing came into my head about when we were young. But maybe I shouldn't have mentioned Robbie McClelland. Only there's no harm in it now, is there?" Alice pleaded.

"No harm at all," Charlotte said heavily. "Because I

am old now. Whether we like it or not, Alice, we're both old, nearly fifty and past all use as women because we've been both of us wasted. And I don't see why. I never did see why. I never looked long ago to fall in love with Robbie. It just happened. But to be shown such a thing—to know how perfect it would be and then it not allowed. Whose fault was that? Robbie's or mine or whose? And you. Alice, why did you get that nervous breakdown, you who were so bright and gay always? If I could see any path through it from the beginning, I've often thought I could bear it all better. And why could I not bear John Conlon a son to get the farm as he wanted? As it is, John and Isa would be far happier without me in the house. Sometimes I hate them, Alice. It frightens me, the hate I feel for them both."

"Maybe, Charlotte, you shouldn't say such things to me. I don't want to hear them," Alice said. "You never know what I'll come out with. It's not safe to tell me anything."

"Safe! What do I want to be safe for? But I'll not burden you. Poor Alice, I've always loaded you with my troubles. And your own were too much for you and not a whisper of them did I ever hear when we were young. Nor even yet do I know what broke you."

"Oh, you know about the rats," Alice said reproachfully. "I told you about the rats. I told everybody about the rats."

"Yes, I know about the rats," Charlotte soothed her.

Alice had been working in a shop in the town, but after a year there she was brought home in great secrecy and there was a general whisper that she was "not quite right." They remembered that her mother's people had a queer streak in them—that cousin of hers who had committed suicide by holding his face down in a couple of

inches of a pool under the willow trees in his lane. "It's rest she needs. Just rest. Plenty of rest," her father emphasized to Charlotte. For some reason that year the district was overrun with rats. They galloped in great rushes in the roof space under the thatch above the unplastered ceiling of Alice's bedroom. They swung down by their claws in the netting wire that her father had fixed over her window and gnawed at the mesh. When poison was laid they swarmed down from the eaves in solid hordes seeking water and their carcasses were shoveled into pits. For weeks after they had been cleared, the house stank of pollution. Coming from the security of her own strong slated house Charlotte's eyes had been wide with horror every time she visited Alice in that room on her high lumpy bed. But that was years ago; the rats had gone. Her body had grown strong again and her hair shone red and the brown circles under her eyes had faded. Only her mind refused to meet things anymore.

"When my father was alive he shook his stick and shouted at them when I screamed," Alice said, repeating her story about the rats. "They were afraid of him. They would just glare at him for a minute and then they'd slink away. Sometimes he shot them out in the yard and they screamed instead of me. That frightened me more than me screaming."

"Don't talk about it," Charlotte urged for her own sake. "You'll only upset yourself."

"You see," Alice said dolefully. "Nobody'll listen. Nobody likes to hear about them. Even you."

"Oh, it's not that, Alice." Charlotte hastened to deny it, blaming herself for her self-absorption. "I was afraid it would not be good for you. But sure you have no rats now."

"Indeed I have. They scuffle away behind the walls all

night," Alice insisted. "That's why I came out this evening in the rain. There was one big one stepping down into the room and he wouldn't get out of my way— cheeky as you please. I asked him where he thought he was going, but he wouldn't budge so I came away and left him." A lorry horn blew behind them and they stepped into the grass at the side until the headlamps cut through the long glitter of rain and passed. "Do you know, Charlotte," Alice resumed reflectively, "I think I like a few rats being there. I'd be lonely without them. I'd miss them."

Charlotte took a quick look sideways at her, excited, hopeful. Anxious to say the right thing she spoke slowly: "If a woman has a child whinging everlastingly, fretting in pain and illness without any possible cure, you'd think she should be relieved if it died and was at peace. But I remember your mother holding your little brother's body and crying that she'd double all his pain and hers to have him back because her arms were curved with nursing him and wouldn't hang empty at her sides." She stopped, not knowing what harm she had done nor why she should say such a thing. "It's emptiness I'm afraid of too," she said loudly, to eradicate the rest, but Alice kept her eyes down on the road.

"I never had a child," she said and Charlotte took her arm.

"No, Alice. Neither had I." They pushed up the dark wet hill in silence and waited at the top till their breathing slowed again.

"I'll go on now by myself," Alice said. "I left the light turned low. I can see it from here." She pointed to the glimmer in the hollow and walked toward it.

"Good night, Alice," Charlotte called cheerfully after her again when the stumbling footsteps were distant.

"God help you," she said low, "with your rats for company." She stood looking down on the insatiably suckling plain, her knuckles gleaming wet clutching the lopsided coat under her chin. "And I—what do I go back to? A cracked lamp and a kicked bitch—a bitch that's kicked only when I'm there, and a man that's angry only when I'm there, and a sister-in-law that's peevish only when I'm there." She could feel the hard heaving of a rebellion that for twenty years had seemed alternately to burst inside her ribs and crush them outside with iron hoops. Alarmed, she cried out, "I'm resigned," and waited for it to subside. "I'm resigned, resigned, resigned, I tell you," she whispered urgently. "Oh, dear God, why don't You hear me, and believe me, and make it be true!" A wind passed over the plain, twitching the empty sleeve of her coat. It scurried bright drops from the hedges and pressed sighing on the green grass, turning it gray for a moment in passing.

Waiting till the quiver in her legs would cease, Charlotte sat down on a smooth hump on the ditch where on warm evenings couples had laughed threading ripe strawberries. Three fields off, a hurricane lamp bobbed round a house. She watched it, knowing each step that was taken in and out of each shed in the yard; she could almost hear the slight creak its handle made keeping time with the man's movements. She smiled, letting her eyelids droop, and through her lashes the round blob of light grew cat's whiskers for her amusement. *There was so much grace between Robbie and me*, she thought, *and he didn't lose it all. If I could have stayed with him I wouldn't have got like this. He is good.* The thought was always on the threshold of her mind, but since her engagement to John Conlon she had thrust it away in panic and walled herself up against it. Now she was tired; she let it

lie. Her sorrow that had shriveled and wizened in the
drought of resentment swelled as she allowed herself re-
gret. The lamp disappeared and then shone, a steady
speck at a small back window. Tears for their loneliness
poured down her cheeks, full quiet tears that would have
drained her of all bitterness, but fear of pain on tenderness made her turn her mind to the point that calloused
her most.

This evening, her sister-in-law, goaded, had said,
"Isn't it a good thing after all you had no children to take
out your temper on?"

And Charlotte had flailed herself: "Oh, yes, it's a
good thing to taunt me with—you and John. Every other
month, for years, 'You're not looking too well,
Charlotte,'" she mimicked viciously. "'Why don't you go
up to the doctor and see is there anything wrong? Why
don't you go and let the doctor have a look at you!' Oh,
yes, let them all have a look at me! Let them all talk in
ugly hoarse whispers and watch me! Let them all see that
I'm old."

John growled in all his surliness, "Well, you *are* old—
too old to have children. Give up talking about it."

It was then that Alice interrupted: "You weren't old,
Charlotte, when you used to roll under barbed wire to
gather flowers in the fields. Do you remember Robbie
McClelland helping you out of the briars and laughing at
you for pulling handfuls of weeds? 'I'll bring them up by
the barrowful,' he said, 'and see how your father likes
that—eh, Charlotte O'Brian?'"

Charlotte's grip on her coat loosened so that it fell
back off her head and in the thick rain her face softened
seeing the poppies and cornflowers and bachelor's but-
tons she'd arranged in old jugs in her house. Sometimes
the petals lay scarlet and golden, soft blue and pink on

the scrubbed flags of the floor. She had been so joyous while she gradually became aware of Robbie that her father, not knowing its cause, laughed leniently at her absentmindedness: "For a sensible girl with a head on your shoulders, you've precious little wit these days."

Before she had faced the possibility, Robbie proposed marriage. He had pulled up by the roots an unwieldy stalk of ladyfingers and, chuckling, he picked off the cool pink bells and decorated her fingers with them. Then he held open her red work-roughened palms, crisscrossed where they had pressed into the grass, and smiled at them. His warm brown eyes when he said, "We'd better get married, Charlotte, you and me," made her say yes with no thought, just awe. But when he drew her to her feet and said, "We'll go now and see your father," she held back.

"Oh, no," she said, "he'd be wild. We'll not tell him till you've turned."

He tightened his hold on her hands till they stood close together, his face above hers. "I'm not turning, Charlotte," he said softly, "but I'll marry you in your chapel even though my poor father will turn in his Presbyterian grave." He laughed down at her and she laughed back, but uncertainly. A half-inkling that this sweetness together was nothing more than an interlude made her insist on their keeping it secret a little longer. It was during that time that their love tangled them both beyond all possible thought of separation.

She talked little, being content in his presence. He was full of plans for his farm, new ideas that he had read in books, and while he talked about these things his voice was detached and firm. Then he would laugh with excitement in being with her and call her his dove in the clefts of the rock, in the secret places of the stairs. A little

breathlessly she asked once, "Did you make that up?" and he put his arms round her and went on: "Thou hast ravished my heart with one of thine eyes, with one chain of thy neck. Thy lips are like a thread of scarlet and the roof of thy mouth like the best wine that goeth down sweetly, causing the lips of those that are asleep to speak."

"Where did you get all those words?" she asked afterward, and he hugged her. "They're all in the Bible, Charlotte—best book there is in the world for courting out of." She looked incredulous and he teased her: "So there's something my little infallible Papish doesn't know." His tenderness toward her made her wonder how she could hold such happiness, but that night she was uneasy. And then the neighbors began to notice.

"The disgrace of it!" her father said. "An O'Brian to marry a Protestant."

"Presbyterian," Robbie corrected him. "And there's a brave bit of disgrace in a McClelland marrying a Roman Catholic and in the chapel too!"

Her father glowered at him but then he admitted, "Aye, I can see that. Could ye not—?" He looked from Robbie to Charlotte's apprehensive face and gave in. "No, I see you couldn't do without each other." Charlotte's lips had parted with unbelieving joy that it was as smooth as this when her father demanded, "You'll sign the promises?"

And Robbie, startled, answered back, "I'll sign nothing." Her father explained with a patient exasperation that he'd have to sign a paper promising that Charlotte should have freedom to practice her religion and that all the children should be brought up Catholics. "I'll sign nothing," Robbie repeated stubbornly and went home.

For weeks Charlotte refused to face the finality of

that. They continued to meet, but the delight they brought each other now had a hard black wall of desperation round it. Not understanding, he tried to persuade her. "Ah, Charlotte think of it. If you bore me a child, could I cross you? Your child and mine and would I raise trouble in you over it? Don't you know I'd let you have your way over their religion?"

"Then why won't you sign?" she asked tearfully.

"I'll sign nothing for your priests," he said flatly. "I'll promise you anything, because I love you, because I want you for my wife, but I'll sign nothing for any priest. I couldn't do it, Charlotte."

"Well, then, that's just bigotry," she said.

"Good God, Charlotte, and what's yours!" he exclaimed. "Don't you see how much I give in? My father and his father before him were elders in the Middle Church and I'm ready to go into a Roman Catholic chapel and marry you whatever way they do it there, and have my children with my name and my land brought up Roman Catholics to please you. And you won't even let me off signing some document as if my word wasn't good enough for you."

"Oh, for me it is good enough. For I would ask nothing." Charlotte put her hands on his arms. "But they will not marry us unless you sign. It's the rule."

He looked down at her for a minute and then he said, "Look, come into the house and I'll get down the big Bible and I'll swear on it whatever you want." She shook her head, unable to make any words come, and seeing her distress he smiled gently and made fun of her. "What, not even the good Bible I've courted you out of? You like the Bible, you know. Ah, don't make yourself unhappy, love, don't!" He ended it for that evening. Once, and only once, he said hard, holding her to him,

"We'll get married in the Middle Church and no diffi-
culties made. And we'll be married before God, and who
else matters?" She looked at him in alarm, pulled away,
and ran home.

They parted. There was half a mile between her father's farm and his. She could not go to the church nor to
the shop nor to the post without a longing dread that she
might see him, and when she did, her body trembled so
that she staggered, walking. In the wild suffocation of
her desire she was besieged by that offer of a Presbyterian wedding. Terrified lest she should give way, she
asked the priest's advice. "Could you go someplace else
for a while?" he asked and she went to an aunt on the
other side of the lough for a few months. But she made
no effort to renew her life and returned to the comfort of
the reserved affection of her people and the handling of
familiar things. "Laugh more," the priest told her. "A
good laugh is more useful than prayer sometimes," and
she smiled wanly. Robbie and laughter had been so
bound up together that being deprived of one she
grudged the other. Then Alice fell ill and her plight
frightened Charlotte.

So that when John Conlon presented himself to her
father, she contracted a halfhearted engagement with
him. She took no interest in him, but the solid bulk of the
man seemed a form of bulwark against herself. She hesi-
tated to close the door finally against Robbie and, aware
of that, John was diffident. Besides, he was content with
his mother and sister; there was no strength in his feeling
for Charlotte, she knew. So they delayed too long and
their bitterness and sense of failure drove her to gibing at
him, and him to roughness with her. They had no children.

Charlotte had no child, Catholic or Presbyterian. John

Conlan had no one to inherit his through-other sixty acres. Robbie McClelland had model piggeries, an orchard just maturing of carefully selected dessert apples, the best dairy herd in the district. (He'd changed over from beef in the middle of the war, when having driven thirty Herefords to the boat for England he could find no shop would sell him a pound of sausages to bring home for his tea. Charlotte smiled remembering the talk of this.) It would all be up for auction when he died.

Her tired eyes closed, shutting out the speck of light she'd concentrated on, and her head drooped on her shoulder in dreamy sadness. Years ago she had twisted and sobbed and said in despair, "I can't bear it. I can't. Dear Lord, You'll have to do something about it." Well, she *had* borne it, she thought. There wouldn't be much more to bear.

She dozed for a second until a sudden violence in the rain beating on her head wakened her. And in her wakening she saw clearly that she had not borne it. As surely as Alice had escaped into vacancy so had she hidden in bitterness, offering no more than a sour husk of herself to everyone since Robbie. Appalled at the harm she had done, she crouched forward. Poor Isa, who had ministered always to John and would have to her, shuffled now to show how little she craved. And John, whom she blamed for his stamping importance, had never heard one word of affection or sympathy from her, nothing but hard rancor.

"Dear Lord, what will I do?" She lifted her face open-eyed to the rain that stung her so that her lashes quailed at its force. It battered through her dress to her arms and her breast and her thighs, stirring her to urgency. She got to her feet, gathering her coat round her; there were things she could do for them when she put her mind to

it. Then she paused to put on her coat straight, buttoning it properly, and to smooth back her hair. Soaking wet it was; what would people say about her streeling round the countryside like this? She hurried down the hill, feeling an excitement and a timidity that made her laugh at herself: "It's not seemly in one of my age."

First she'd call in the shop at the head of the lane and buy a new globe for the lamp. She had no money with her, but it was no matter—she'd take something on credit for once. And then she'd polish it with crumpled newspaper till it was clear and shining on its own account. They could do with a new wick too. She'd put it in tonight even though she had to do it with her back to darkness, kneeling by the fire. The light would be thin to begin with, wavering on the ceiling, until the oil soaked through. Then the flame would grow broad and rich and the heartening brightness would come steadily down the walls, even though it must leave patches of shadow, soft natural shadow.

Ruth

Between the high thorn hedges the road held on the steep hill all the heat there had been in the overcast day. The woman on the first bicycle wavered, glanced behind her, then bent over the handlebars and pushed zigzagging for another few yards before she had to yield and stand waiting for the heat to recede from her face. She made a show of surprise as the wirier woman rode up to her.

"I didn't know you were behind me at all, Mrs. Mc-Corry," she said. "I don't know am I getting fatter or is it the touch of rheumatism I have, but this hill gets steeper every summer."

They stood looking back at the height they had come and then turned and walked up the other half of the hill,

leaning hard over their handlebars. When they finished climbing they talked of the weather and when the binder was booked, until they came to the corner of a side road.

"Well, Mrs. McCorry, I turn in here."

The fat woman nodded a farewell, but "Then you'll have my company, Mrs. Gormley" the other retorted, and they both laughed politely, and did not look at each other.

Presently Mrs. Gormley said, "I'm going to McGreevy's to inquire after Ruth. I suppose you're doing the same. What I was wondering was—does it look well to see two of us arriving together? What way will Mrs. McGreevy look at it? Does it seem maybe as if we were gossiping together and decided to come prying?"

Their eyes met in agreement and they waited, considering, until the suggestion of a breeze ruffled the skirt of Mrs. McCorry's brown floral dress, and she asked, "Did you hear anything more at all?"

"Not a thing," she was told, and slowly they both began wheeling their bicycles on toward McGreevy's.

"It's a mystery," Mrs. McCorry said, shaking her head.

"Wouldn't you wonder why such things should happen to a decent well-doing family," Mrs. Gormley said, and immediately Mrs. McCorry confirmed.

"A decent steadfast man, Eivear McGreevy, and all his people the same. Never would see you in want for labor or tools but he'd give you what you need without a word. But no matter what anybody says, I hold there's something queer about Rose Killen. Oh, I'm not saying anything. A quiet woman too, and can mind her own business, but there's just that wee something." Mrs. Gormley was silent, her expression troubled, and Mrs. McCorry went on, "Where did Sally come from if there

wasn't an odd streak somewhere that we never heard about? And wasn't there badness there too?"

"Ah, no," Mrs. Gormley said, her voice tender. "God rest her, poor Sally. Nobody could blame her for she wasn't responsible, no more than a child. The way she came up the hill from the doctor's that day, telling everybody she met that she was going to have a wee baby, and she all delighted and charmed, and the poor mother saying no more than 'Hush, love. There's no need to tell people. Keep it a secret, pet.'"

Mrs. McCorry's mouth was thin. "Hm," she said, and after a few yards could restrain herself no longer. "Many a one would have broken her back on her, and I don't know that it wouldn't have been right. They have a kind of cuteness, people like her. But I'll not speak ill of the dead."

"Poor Sally," Mrs. Gormley repeated. "She had the whitest skin, like buttermilk—arms and legs white the way I've never seen. I always had a feeling that if ever you touched her it would leave a black bruise. You'd have known to look at her she wasn't right, but it was nice to look at her just the same, with that big smile for everybody her eye rested on."

"She brought disgrace on her people," Mrs. McCorry snapped.

"She did," Mrs. Gormley agreed, but placidly.

"A lot of use it was giving out that she'd died of appendicitis and hiding the child in a home. Sure there wasn't one in the countryside but knew the truth. And still they had it to do, I suppose," Mrs. McCorry conceded. "It saved us all from shame. And Eivear McGreevy couldn't live without his decency and his dignity. Only why had they to go and destroy it all when people had nearly forgotten? Taking the child home with-

out a word of excuse as to where the lump of a girl had come from! Now look how she repays them—just disappears. Oh, well, that's how it is when things get out of hand," she concluded hurriedly as they turned a corner of the road and saw McGreevy's house. It was well out of earshot, but the door stood open and a small bent woman was brushing off the griddle into the hedge with a turkey's wing. A little black dog licked up the flour as it sifted to the ground through the lower twigs, but when the bicycles came into the yard it crouched, growling and shivering, against Mrs. McGreevy's legs, so that she turned and smiled a welcome.

"Mrs. Gormley, I'm that pleased to see you. And Mrs. McCorry." She patted the dog to quieten it, but it snapped, and she said, "Oh, dear," apologetically, "it's nervous, poor thing. But come in, I've just brought back Eivear's and Arthur's tea things from the field and we'll have peace for ours."

"Where did you get the wee dog?" Mrs. Gormley asked when they sat down. "I thought it was a big sheepdog Eivear had."

"Oh, so it is," Mrs. McGreevy answered, "but this one came and adopted us. It slunk round the bottom of the yard for long enough and I threw scraps to it. Then last week she decided to come in. Mostly she feels quite at home now. She doesn't belong to anybody round here."

Mrs. McCorry asked, "What good will it be to you?" and Mrs. McGreevy answered, "None, Mrs. McCorry," both speaking levelly, but Mrs. Gormley, feeling their dislike, shifted her chair on the tiles and cleared her throat.

She was not quick enough to speak, however, for Mrs. McCorry said, "I hope it will not repay you like

some," and Mrs. McGreevy took up the challenge without any sign of discomfort.

"It's Ruth you mean. She owed us nothing."

"Nothing!" Mrs. Gormley burst out indignantly, but Mrs. McGreevy prevented her saying any more.

"She was twelve when we took her in. She worked her way with us for eight years. If she had been a servant I'd have had to pay her." Her voice was matter-of-fact and both visitors looked at her quiet face and doubt wavered in theirs.

"But she was one of the house," Mrs. Gormley protested, unsure. "Every girl works about the house."

"She was my own flesh and blood, Mrs. Gormley," and the words spoken for the first time caused excitement in the other two. "She was my own flesh and blood and Eivear's. And we gave her a roof and food and clothing from she was twelve."

"But what more could you give her?" Mrs. Gormley asked, puzzled. "What more was there to give?"

"Love." The word stood alone and strange in the kitchen. In the ensuing silence the women began to wonder had it been said at all, or had Mrs. McGreevy ignored the questions entirely? She sat looking across the fire, her raised head young and proud in the shadow. Then she turned to them vehemently. "Do you see that wee dog there? If it cowers away from us, nervous, or grows surly and growls, I speak all soothing to it. So does Eivear. And strokes its ears and softens his voice and goes on saying, 'Poor Curly, poor wee Curly,' until it sits up close to his legs. And Arthur will feed it bits of his dinner right here at the table. But when Ruth came here eight years ago, did we do for the child what we do for the dog? We did not. It's a safe thing to show affection to a dog. It doesn't refuse it, or, if it does, your pride isn't hurt, but if

a child snubs you, that's a wound, and people like us don't risk it."

"Aye, well, you're only upsetting yourself, Mrs. McGreevy," Mrs. Gormley soothed. "We'll not talk about it anymore."

Mrs. McGreevy looked at her sadly. "And why?" she asked. "Why do we not talk about things? Because that's another risk. It's giving a wee bit of yourself, nearly like loving. It's safer saying nothing, give nothing, love nothing. God Almighty, God Almighty, don't I know." She rocked. "That's the way I've lived my life, and I've lost my child and my grandchild, and I've never found my husband or my son."

"Mrs. McGreevy—Rose—stop it now." Mrs. Gormley's voice was sharp. "It's not your fault, the trouble you're in, and getting into a state will only do harm, for you'll be sorry afterward you spoke out so much."

"It *is* my fault," she lamented. "There was no call for me to model myself on everybody round me."

"You can't judge everybody by yourself, Rose Killen," Mrs. McCorry snapped.

"I can judge by comparing my face with theirs. I can see the hard lines at the sides of their mouths, Mrs. McCorry, and the strain in their eyes." She became wistful. "I've seen in the town an odd girl with a face that you'd know was in love. I've seen women's faces when they looked at small children. I've seen Sally's face. She had no pride. It wasn't in her to protect herself, and because she loved me and I loved her. No credit to me."

"She couldn't have had a better mother," Mrs. Gormley said, on surer ground now. "And she's happy, blessed, where she is. You couldn't worry or grieve over her, Rose. Isn't she well off compared to aging lonely, maybe without you?"

"God knows," Mrs. McGreevy said simply in the quiet sadness that fell easily on her. "She was the only girl that I had and I did all I could, but you see what happened. By myself I was no use to her when she grew up a bit. Often I've wondered, if her father and brother had shown her affection would it have made any difference? But sure I don't know. And I don't blame them. For Eivear was ashamed that a child of his should be wanting, and Arthur knew that such a thing in the family sets him to one side and cuts into his life. He'll never find one in this place to marry him. Poor Arthur. I never blamed him when his eyes wouldn't meet Sally's but slid away from her, awkward looking. And Eivear. Ach, I suppose he couldn't go against his nature."

"Sally's dead twenty years, Mrs. McGreevy," Mrs. Gormley said. "It's not good to be still turning it over in your mind."

"You're right, Mrs. Gormley," she agreed. "But I can't help puzzling over Sally. It's different with Ruth. If anything happens to Ruth I'll know who to blame. Nobody but myself."

"Oh, dear," Mrs. Gormley said. "Mrs. McCorry, we're only doing harm sitting here."

"It's her business. We can't see what she has in her mind," Mrs. McCorry answered, and they sat on in uncomfortable separation.

"It's nothing secret I have in my mind." Mrs. McGreevy's voice was tired. "You all know what I gave out at Sally's funeral. I never even saw the child or thought of anything except to keep Sally from gossip and shame. But why didn't Eivear tell me it was nonsense and to take the child home and rear it?"

"Maybe he felt the same as yourself," Mrs. Gormley suggested.

"Maybe he did," she agreed. "I don't know." She moved her hands over her aproned knees. "I dreamed once, a wee while after she died, that I was crying and he came to me and put his arm round my shoulder, Eivear did. And that I leaned my head against him and he stroked my face and said I'd had it hard but the baby would console me. I dreamed it, I say. Eivear hadn't it in him to do such a thing. It was all mixed up in the dream, and the baby was Sally, but when I wakened I had it in my head that we should take Ruth home."

"Well, you did take her home and you were good to her and she'll come back, I'm certain sure. Won't she, Mrs. McCorry?"

Mrs. Gormley fussed, but Mrs. McGreevy refused to be halted. She spoke slowly, remembering: "Do you know how long I lay beside Eivear night after night, and sat opposite him day after day, before I got my tongue round the words to ask him could we take Ruth? Do you know how long? And not one of you came to me all that time and hinted at what we should do. Not one of you spoke, and it was eleven years."

"Now, what on earth could we say?" Mrs. Gormley protested. "Indeed I thought you had done right. You'd your husband and son to think of."

"But you all knew. That was the thing. There was no sense in hiding what was known, no sense at all. You talked among yourselves but there wasn't one would speak out to me."

"Ach, we couldn't," Mrs. Gormley said flatly. "Neither could you to anyone else."

"No." Mrs. McGreevy's voice lifted and lightened. "That's what I say. That's what's wrong with us all. Don't talk about it. Be safe. Cautious."

"It's not a bad thing maybe," Mrs. McCorry put in.

Mrs. McGreevy looked at her steadily, smiling a little, and Mrs. McCorry's eyes dropped and she fidgeted.

"It's the easy way for people outside, all right," Mrs. McGreevy said, the smile disappearing. "But when it comes into a house, it's hard. We're not any different from the rest, Eivear and I, sure we're not, Mrs. Gormley. He's a good husband and he's suffered with this maybe more than me. But wouldn't it have eased him too if he'd talked and not been so stern with himself always?"

"He wouldn't like to hear you airing private matters the way you're doing now, I'm thinking," Mrs. McCorry snapped.

"No, I expect not," she said humbly. "But I've more than I can stand by myself. I hope you never discover that there comes a time when it's harder to keep things in than to let them out."

"Hush, Rose," Mrs. Gormley soothed again as she let her distress shake her. "Maybe you should pour yourself another cup of tea."

Mrs. McGreevy fell in with her suggestion politely, like a visiting child, and when she spoke again her voice was calm. "All those years I nerved myself day after day to say, 'Eivear, what would you think of taking Sally's child out of the home and bringing her here?' And when I did say it, he was putting on his big coat to go away up to see to the hill cattle, and all he answered was 'If you think it best, Rose. You need help, maybe, round the house.' Then he went off. There was a kindness in the words themselves, don't you see," she appealed to Mrs. Gormley. "A kindness for me and a kindness for the child, but he said it hard in his ordinary voice, and I was set back because I'd imagined some comfort and light-

ness would come from saying it. I'd be afraid I took out my disappointment on the child when she came."

"Now, indeed you did no such thing," Mrs. Gormley said indignantly. "You welcomed her and you were good to her, and you'll see it the right way round in a day or two. It's likely just that Ruth didn't relish everybody knowing all about her here—the way you said about Arthur. She'd have a better chance in one of the big towns in England, they tell me."

"Oh, yes, there's all that." Mrs. McGreevy nodded emphatically. "She'd have had to go sometime if she'd wanted to have any life of it. It's that—" She stopped, bothered. "Ach, she's poor, Ruth, and empty, and how is she to know what is love or friendship, and not be grasping out for the wrong thing when she's lonely? She's just turned twenty."

"Ruth's not soft," Mrs. McCorry said. "She'll manage to look after herself. She could buy and sell us all with cuteness."

"You're wrong," Mrs. McGreevy said sadly, "but I can't blame you, for that's how she looked always."

"A harmless wee girl was all she was, Mrs. McGreevy. Quiet, and kept to herself, that was all," Mrs. Gormley said in her defense.

"Aye, she kept to herself, Mrs. Gormley, you're right." Mrs. McGreevy sighed. "That's what it was. But the mistake I made was in expecting another Sally."

Both women's eyebrows flew up, startled, and Mrs. Gormley exclaimed, "Oh, no!"

"I don't mean wanting, like Sally. No, I never thought of that," Mrs. McGreevy explained, "but loving and smiling." She smiled tenderly herself, and her whole body relaxed in the warmth of her recollection so that her voice was full of pity when she went on. "When wee cold Ruth

came through the door and looked at me stiff and hard and wouldn't give me more than a bit of a handshake, I didn't know what to do or where to turn. Many and many a time I'd say to myself it was my own fault for leaving her so long without one belonging to her. But I couldn't bring myself to be fond of her. Ach, I never was nasty to her, but I never went and put my arms round her. You saw what she was like. She gave no trouble, not for a single second all the eight years she was here, but she gave no happiness either, and I don't think she got any herself from us. It's been a dour house since Sally died. God knows what will happen to Ruth."

"She's pretty," Mrs. Gormley said, and Mrs. McGreevy smiled, but shook her head. "I thought that too, when I saw her first, except for looking a bit pinched and blue, and I thought a fortnight in our house, with good food, would take the close sharp corners from her face. But she didn't change much, not even her hair. Nothing but wee wisps of hair she had, really. And her eyes, gray, that she never let soften. It was a face you didn't think good-looking at all when you lived opposite it for a wee while. I don't fault Eivear and Arthur for bothering none with her. It was up to me to make her warm and open, and I didn't, and she's gone and if she comes back at all I'd be afraid she'd be damaged more than ever."

Mrs. Gormley stood up and carefully shook a few crumbs from her lap into the hearth. "Ah well, we'll hope she'll come to no harm and get a job and be happy. I'm going now or they'll be wondering what's happened to me. Will you be with me, Mrs. McCorry?"

Mrs. McGreevy rose too, stiffly, and in the brighter light of the doorway she looked exhausted. "I'm sorry," she said. "I've talked too much about my trouble, and

never even asked how you all were. And I know if you sat till bedtime I'd keep going over and over the same things if I didn't watch myself. For I've found myself doing that in my head till I was nearly astray. How's Hugh getting on at the college, Mrs. McCorry?" she asked.

"The best at all," Mrs. McCorry answered, pleased. "And Rita too—she can bake things she's learning at this class now would make your mouth water."

They bade goodbye when they had wheeled their bicycles down the yard to the road, and Mrs. McGreevy turned back into her own house.

Then Mrs. McCorry burst out. "Well, that was an exhibition."

"Poor Mrs. McGreevy," Mrs. Gormley said, "She's in a bad way."

"I wonder why she came over all that." Mrs. McCorry's pedaling slowed. "Would you say there's something worse maybe than we think—something she's trying to hide?"

"Oh, not a thing. She said a lot of truth."

"A lot of snash and blathers and not a word but what's been common property for years," Mrs. McCorry said, and then demanded, "Did we hear where Ruth's gone?"

"No," Mrs. Gormley said thoughtfully, "no. Right enough. We didn't hear much about that. But maybe she didn't know, like she said."

"Huh!" Mrs. McCorry scoffed. "If she didn't know she wouldn't have had to start on all that ancient history to take our minds off it. Oh, Ruth isn't the only cute one." She looked sideways at Mrs. Gormley. "Would you feel comfortable visiting in that house again?" she asked quietly and Mrs. Gormley took a long time to answer.

"I liked Mrs. McGreevy. And then there was always cause to be sorry for her," but she sounded uncertain.

"Ah, well, we asked no questions and we were told no lies," Mrs. McCorry said glibly. "Oh, she's deep, Rose Killen. But it'll puzzle my mind tonight to think what she's keeping in behind all that spate of talk. There's some plan, you know, some reason. There must be."

And they were at the top of the hill so there could be no more talk, nothing but the easy whir of the bicycles creating a little breeze that scuffled the fine dust at the margin of the road while the hedges remained still in the closeness of the evening.

Flags and Emblems

In a hollow in the sand dunes on the far side of the town the girl lay dreaming. Her pink linen dress was crumpled and her warm cheeks were brown with the sun. Hazy with heat the waves of sound could have been strong breakers on the shingle or cheers in the breeze from the town or only the beat of blood in her ears. Then she heard shots; she was sure she heard shots and her eyes were alarmed as she listened, her head tall on her neck. She parted the whins and plowed through the dry sand toward the sea, bare-legged, her sandals in her hand. On the broad stretch of the inlet only a trickle of water remained. On the edge, remnant of the backwash of a boat, a bubble of froth formed and drifted uncertainly out toward the current for the sea. Another fol-

lowed, and another, each single, untouched, bumped now and then by a ripple, a feeble unending procession. Her sudden energy sucked back into the whirling impatience within her, she stood watching, while her briar-scratched feet sank down where the weak waves receded. Then she sighed, pushed her limp hair back from her cheeks, and turned in toward the town.

The flags were all hanging still, their colors softened beside rose brick and flaming glass reflecting a bar of red below a cloud at the mountain. Down at the railway station where the guarded parade had gone, white puffs strayed across the sky, which was cheap chocolate-box blue. Knots of women gossiped to prolong sensation in the littered street. All day, deafened with drums beaten loudly in greeting to sleek royal cars, crushed and dazzled with the brightness of silk and gold braid, they had flapped little triangles of bunting or ranted at home against them. They brushed against the girl, not noticing her, and through the flitters of their excitement she could see her own emptiness.

Her father's shop was shuttered; the house was closed tight, door bolted, the catch on the window. She rapped and was drawn into the dark hall by her aunt, plucking off burdensome glasses. They disturbed the usual arrangement of her hair over her ears so she tucked and patted it.

"Was there shooting? I thought I heard shots," the girl said, but her aunt hushed her to talk in whispers. "It was maybe an echo. Your father's in bad form. Don't cross him now. I don't know what we're to do." Her defenseless face wobbled.

"Because father's in a temper!" the girl exclaimed and the cold weight that had all day been heavy in her breast made her voice mocking.

"You'll maybe agree I have cause this time," her father shouted, his lower lip protruding in bitterness.

"Somebody tramped on your toes, I suppose," she scoffed and he glared at her with the hatred that lodged often under his drooped lids because the world didn't please him.

"What's the matter?" she asked more gently and he muttered, "It's Fergus," and put his head down on his hand.

"What about him?" she asked, quiet in fear. "Did they give him the sack when he wouldn't line up at the works to cheer?"

"I wish to God they had," her father said. "I could be proud of that—a man standing up for his principles. Then maybe that wife of his would take herself back to the Unionist brood that she came from."

"Poor Rachel," her aunt intervened. "Would you separate husband and wife?" She rattled the ashes in the grate so that the whole sunset was obscured by spinning dust and then wiped ineffectually at her glasses.

"I would separate Fergus from anyone that made a disgrace of him and count myself justified too." He thumped his fist on his knee.

"Nobody could make a disgrace of Fergus," the girl flared. "What are you creating a scene about? Some footling thing that matters to no one!"

"How would you like to see your brother out walking the streets this day with a flag—a Union Jack in honor of our royal guests?" His sarcasm was thick on his tongue but the girl's quick laughter choked him. "What are you laughing at, you fool?" he raged at his daughter.

Not even his surliness could suppress her spurt of merriment. "Oh, Father, don't be silly," she said. "Fergus waving flags! That's what I'm laughing at. You

would do it yourself before he would. Don't ever let him hear you believed such a thing."

His face was a twist of anger when she began, but the old lines fell back into place before she had finished and he said with slow deliberation, as if each word would not leave his lips, "Out for a walk with the young lad he was, and a wee flag in the child's hand and the wife looking after them from the door."

"Oh . . ." the girl said, realizing that only in this way could the news be true. "Who told you?"

"Half the town," he answered. Then he added, "Owen Devlin met them head on just past his gate and he didn't even tell the child to put the flag in his pocket then."

"No, he wouldn't."

The girl shook her head and her father said "Ach!" hard in irritation. "Why wouldn't he and not have Devlin sneering at him: 'We'll hardly see you at the club tonight. Who'll we get for secretary now?'"

The girl suffered for a second the slight on her brother's self-esteem; the father writhed at the blow to his own. The aunt tried to divert them: "But it wasn't his fault. It was Rachel's. Blame Rachel. Her people were loyalist always. She had given Michael the flag to carry and Fergus wouldn't wish to go against her."

"And why wouldn't he?" the father blazed. "Lord God, before I'd disgrace my name and my people I'd have him rip the flag from the child's hand and hurl it in her face and if she didn't like it she could leave him. A man's got to live up to his ideals."

The girl looked sad. "Is that the way an idealist should act?" She considered. "Perhaps it's because his ideals dignify his mind that Fergus is gentle, unlike most men around here. Dead words and empty venom are all I

can hear in what passes for idealism nowadays. You, now," she said coldly, "is there not in your rage an envy of those shops that made money on ribbons and flags while you couldn't, and will you lose custom perhaps if people fall out with Fergus?" She hated herself for taunting so cheaply.

"Look out, would you talk to your father like that!" The aunt waved her hands in alarm and then relapsed into self-pity. "The pair of you were out all day and did I once have my foot past the door? No, I've been cooped up in here watching the crowds pushing, until I pulled the blind, only that made the thud of their backs on the windows sound worse with the way they were pressed off the street to let pass the big motorcars and policemen. And then home you two come and I've to listen to bickering and fighting all night. Well, I'll not stay. I'll go to my bed." She rose and began bundling her knitting into its white cloth wrapping.

"Ah, sit your ground," he ordered and she did so meekly. "Damnation take these Unionists," he said out of a few moments' silence, "with their visitors over from England and their flags and their lunches and processions. What right have they to wreck us? And why couldn't he keep to his own sort instead of marrying one of theirs in such a big hurry?"

"Well, he loved her," the girl said.

"Oh ho, listen to that now!" her father mocked. "And she loved him too, did she? And so they lived happy ever after. Is that it? Why does she do this to him then? Shame him? Make a renegade of him!"

"He's not shamed," the girl insisted hotly. "A wife has feelings to be considered; principles haven't. You don't seem to see what courage it took."

"Courage! What use is courage like that?" he said.

"No use indeed." The aunt shook her head. "Poor Rachel. Fergus will never forgive her. He'd save her face outside, but you couldn't expect him to take kindly to her again. It's well she has the child. Poor Fergus that was so busy every night with the Hibernian Hall and the Casement Commemoration Committee and all the rest of them! He'll have nothing now that his evenings with the men are taken away from him. But there's nothing we can do. We may go to our beds; it's dark night."

"It's not time. We'll go no earlier than usual. We'll see this day out if it has ruined us," the father ordered.

"This day, every day. What difference?" the girl said bleakly. She left them and went upstairs to her room and opened her window. The distant lipping whisper on the sand and the sucking puffs of little breezes from the hills taunted her with their lack of violence. She closed her eyes and across the darkness came the staid line of wobbling foam rings that would never reach the open sea. "The shots," she said to herself, remembering. "The shots were only an echo. The fuss of the visit has happened before and will happen again and it is so arranged that nothing happens at all. The only real thing today is between Fergus and Rachel."

In his house in a new street at the edge of the town where the builder's gear was not yet cleared away, her brother sat withdrawn, his mouth set thin. Rachel's hands were clenched together in her lap while her mind scurried from the fear that this blankness between them would continue. Some neighboring child had dropped the flag in the hall and, picking it up, a moment's blind anger against the affairs that kept Fergus from her made her push it into her son's hand and look back defiance at her husband's shock. It was when she saw Owen Devlin

meet them that all her resentment died in sorrow at what she'd done. She realized that she had impaled him, not for one afternoon but, in a small town hoarding memories, for the length of his life. He would suffer for his weakness and she would suffer with him and the knowledge that she shared his expiation would intensify it. She searched his face for some sign of forgiveness, unable to bear it that he should leave her now more alone than ever.

"I'm sorry, Fergus," she said, the ache in her breast and her throat making her voice tremble.

He half-shrugged. "There's nothing to be sorry about," he said without lifting his head from the paper.

Helpless, she would have offered twenty more years of her starvation to have undone the moment's revolt and left him undisturbed, occupied to his own satisfaction. She got up and laid her cheek against his arm, against the ridge under his coat where his shirt sleeve was rolled up in spite of her early insistence that he wear his cuffs neatly linked at the wrist. His body stiffened but she said humbly, "I wish I had not done it."

He drew her to him and she pressed her head against his chest so that the badges in his lapel tangled in her hair and the pen and pencils in his pocket dug hard against her forehead. "I'm very sorry, dear love," she repeated, and he said, "It doesn't matter," gently. He stroked her head as it leaned there and swiftly the wealth that had almost disintegrated in despair through his neglect came to warm stirring life in his arms. They strengthened round Rachel and she lifted her face. "It doesn't matter at all, love," he murmured and she watched his lips, neither aware what words had been spoken, only glad that their tone had been tender. A gust of strong wind round their house rattled their windows, unnoticed by them. Their love grew and engrossed them till they rested together in deep peace.

The Master and the Bombs

"No news of Matthew?"

"Any word of the master?"

They're all asking me, every man and woman in the place, and they look queerly at me when I just say, "No. No news, no word." It's not that they expect me to have heard anything but to have done something, either by myself or with their advice or help. They tell me about the fine man he is and the great teacher and the shame it would be if he got into trouble he didn't deserve. Then they make vague offers. "If there's anything at all we can do, now, let us know," and I promise.

But why must it all depend on me? Why must I decide? I'm a woman. I'm supposed to be passive. I've got three small children; I'm expecting another. At the mo-

ment I'm dull and stupid and slow and my feet swell. I am not going to rush round from parish priest to M.P. to get Matthew out. I could do it, I suppose, for the whole thing is ridiculous. He was never out of the house long enough to belong to any illegal organization. Still, he decided to walk out on us, so I'm going to pretend to respect his decision—I'm leaving it to him. He's the man; let him act like one. Or there's nothing to prevent the men he's been brought up with acting for him. He has a brother down the street with a pub, another a bit out of town with a farm. They're all his people, strangers to me. It's not their fault, they seem kind enough, but I never know what they will do or why they do it, the way I would with people from Belfast. I hear in their talk a cold curiosity, a gathering of gossip, a lack of warmth. But then I have a great lack in myself. If my marriage with Matthew had been happier I might have warmed to his neighbors more, or if I had been among my own people I might have warmed to Matthew more. But there it is.

The school should open on Monday. It will be a bit of a puzzle to everybody if he's not there to open it, but it will be a great relief to Matthew. I don't know if he is as bad at his job as he thinks he is. The people now say he's grand, but some parents and priests have been difficult to deal with and inspectors have criticized him and every time it happens he gets into a state. If he had got the pub or the farm instead of the education, he'd be a far happier man and easier to live with, I suppose. And still, it was because he was a teacher that I talked to him that first time I met him at a dance in Belfast. I have always thought it must be very exciting to be a teacher, to show children how many ways there are of using their minds. Of course people tell me it isn't like that at all, that I don't know what I'm talking about, but I've had teachers

myself who were enthusiastic. Anyway, when Matthew told me he was a teacher I asked him all kinds of questions about it and he thought I had taken a fancy to him and he left me home.

Now when he comes in after a bad day at school and he has a beaten look in those big liquid brown eyes of his, appealing to me for comfort and sympathy, as he has every right to, I'm useless. I feel nothing but revulsion—I have to get away from him, out to a different room, not to breathe the same air that he sighs out of him. All I can do is wait until he has himself in hand again and then tell him to change his job, to take any other work under the sun that wouldn't torment him, even for far less money. We could manage. But he says he can't because of the children. What about the children now? Where is next month's pay to come from? He had no children before he married me; there was nothing to stop him changing then.

That's why I welcomed the holidays, even though there were days I was sure the top of my head must be blown straight off with temper and bits of me stain the ceiling like out of the pressure cooker. He'd just sit there reading the newspaper in front of the fire, letting the fire go out, never giving me any offer of help. Only he'd tut-tut if Margaret and John were fighting or if Margaret put her dirty wee fingers on his trouser leg, so that in the middle of all my washing or baking or the baby's feed I'd have to whirl John and his tricycle out to the front path and Margaret through the back door to her sandpit. Then I'd try to remind myself that men need peace or that his suits had to last him a long time now so that he has to be careful. He'd continue reading the paper, but I'd say he wasn't reading it; there never was enough in any paper to give such long reading.

He must have been sitting there hating me—much more than I hated him because I was busy and I had the baby. It's impossible for me to bathe the baby, to play with her, or indeed to take her on my knee at all and not feel all my irritation melt away. I'd find myself saying, "Look, Matthew. Look at her." Only he never did look in time to catch whatever little unimportant thing she'd done that delighted me. I cannot easily forgive him for ignoring the children, especially now when he has withdrawn every support.

"You can take me away, Officer. I am entirely responsible." That's what he said to those two astonished policemen that called last Wednesday. "Officer"! Like in a silly detective story. And away he went off with them without even turning back into the house to tell me. He didn't know what to say to me of course, since I knew it was all nonsense. The policemen had found bombs or grenades or something like that in the school coal shed. They wanted to know had Matthew seen anyone in particular going in or out. It was a perfectly reasonable question. We live next door to the school, and even though it's been shut all summer Matthew has the keys and goes over now and again to do records and to get peace from the children and me. He wouldn't go near the coal shed—it hasn't been used since Easter and won't again until the children have been thoroughly frozen for a few weeks in late autumn. I was waiting to hear what long-drawn-out account he would give of every passing cyclist that had used the school lavatory—it's a thing annoys him. "You can take me away, Officer. I am entirely responsible." That's what I heard. And he just drops all his own real responsibilities off him—wife, children, work. He escapes from them all to a nice peaceful cell where nobody will expect anything from him, and if he's

brought to court he'll refuse to recognize the court and so he won't have to say anything. It's all so easy. That's what makes me mad. There are times I think I won't let him, that I'll go and tell the authorities that he suffers from delusions or derangement and really cannot be blamed for what he says. Everybody knows he had no hand, act, or part in putting those things there to be a danger to all the children once the school would open. But he wouldn't like to be let home because he's a kind of an idiot. I couldn't do it to him. I don't wish him anything but good. I owe him a lot, poor Matthew, for he's done a lot more for me than ever I do for him.

Looking back, I suppose I should never have married him, but it's easy to forget how unsettled I was then, how empty. And I wanted peace. Well, I got peace. Then, I would have never believed it possible that there could come such a dearth of desire so soon. That old mahogany bed he bought in an auction has always sagged down under his weight at his side and I spend all the warm nights clinging onto my edge so as not to roll down against him. If there was one flicker of love between us that would be a cause for laughing, but there never has been. He never loved me nor did he pretend to, either before or after we married. I had neither love nor respect for him and I never pretended to myself these things would grow. We were both lonely, but we didn't help each other's loneliness; we didn't alter it at all.

We had started writing letters to each other, but his mannered sentences annoyed me and I had stopped. Then one Saturday morning I was downtown and I had that feeling of empty misery I used to have so often. It put black blinkers at the side of my eyes. It wasn't the kind of full sadness you can cry with and get relief; just a feeling of being useless and unwanted and of dwindling

instead of growing. I was doing simple uninteresting work in a dull office, I read bits of silly plays in a play-reading group, I went to an odd dance. My mother had died when we were small; my two brothers had left home, one as a radio officer on a boat, the other to Kenya. I was alone with my father, but he didn't like my interfering with the housekeeping. He had had to do it so long himself he thought his was the only way. He had done his best for us. He had worried that we should be warmly clothed and well fed and into jobs, but all the affection went out of the house when my mother died. It was crowded downtown that Saturday and a po-licewoman was at the pedestrian crossing. I stood among the crowd waiting to cross and it suddenly came to me that it was a very unimportant thing that I was unhappy. I had to put back my head and take breath because the thought came with such force. And when we were let cross I got an excitement out of the pushing two-way jos-tle of people and I felt it mattered only to be alive and to use every bit of one's life, and that the only way I could do that was to have children. Matthew would do better than waiting around till I was past use, because hap-piness was only the froth on the drink and a flat drink would quench thirst just as well as a fizzy one.

And of course I've had odd puffs of happiness—what else makes me lie with a great beaming silly smile on my face just after my babies are born? I'm good at having babies: I practice breathing beforehand, I go to the hospi-tal at the right time, I make no fuss. If I lost control of myself like a few women I've heard in the labor ward and made that awful animal roaring, or even if I whinged and complained, I should be ashamed. I should feel, I sup-pose, as Matthew does about his teaching. But I have found through him that one thing I can do with satisfac-

tion. Another thing: Though I'm lonely still—God knows I was never lonelier—I have a shield for my loneliness. Nobody need know and pity me. Matthew has found no addition to himself in his life with me.

I satisfy his appetites, nothing more, and I'm not even going to do that much longer. This is the last baby I'm having. Four is enough for us if I'm to rear them properly and be warm and sweet and loving as I remember my mother, not always tired and crabbed as I am. Anyway, we haven't really enough money for more even if Matthew doesn't lose his job. So we'll have to talk it over together after this baby is born and come to some arrangement to take care. It's a funny thing: These four were conceived without any love or friendship between us, but we won't be able to stop having babies unless we manage to talk to each other with understanding. Once I get myself screwed up to it I know Matthew will agree in practice, but he might sulk. I've never allowed myself to long for affection between us, but now and again I have seen warmth and kindness in a man's face greeting his wife and her smile welcoming him and I imagine how beautiful it would be if Matthew would say then, "My poor Helen, you've had it hard. You need a rest." I don't think he could manage endearments, but he could manage that. He won't, though—but maybe I could to him when he comes home if I didn't sound too much of a hypocrite: "My poor Matthew, you've had a hard time. Come on and we'll be friends. Don't be out with me any longer." Oh, I'd need to practice being a nice wife to him the way I've practiced to give birth. But the way I am now, I have no energy for anything extra—I've been married five years and this is my fourth child.

You see, I should sympathize with Matthew's running away to prison. I've been doing it all along since my first

pregnancy. It was a different world I discovered. I was placid; I was contented. Nothing penetrated me. I stopped aching for the people who were poor or lost or cold. I read books and couldn't remember a word of them. I sat in company with my hands in my lap, not offering a word to the conversation. At Christmas I was so besotted that instead of talking to Christ in the stable I talked to him as if He were the child moving in my own womb. I would have shared all this with Matthew, but he didn't seem to want to hear, nor to feel the child kicking nor to be seen out with me. So I didn't tell him about my discomforts either, although he saw me limping with the sciatica I have had with each of them. When my legs cramped at night I got up and came downstairs. When the doctor told me I must rest I didn't bother him. He never had the slightest worry passed on to him because he couldn't share my joy, which was so much greater than all the pains I've ever known. Each time, though, when the baby was three or four months old, the numbness began to wear off and the old pins and needles started pestering me again. I don't know what this inner restlessness is I suffer from. I used to think when I'd get married it would go, but it's nothing to do with marriage. I don't understand it. I don't know how to cope with it so I dive back into pregnancy again. Only each time the weariness and worries are greater and now this time I have to search deep to find any joy.

I suppose I'd better go and see Matthew. The thought of all the effort it needs is what has kept me at home—that and the blessed peace we've all enjoyed in the house this week. I'll have to give the children their dinner, clean them up, and park them with somebody and listen to the baby screaming—because that's the stage she's at—when I leave to catch the afternoon bus. I don't

know what time of day or day of the week visiting is allowed. Maybe I should go down to Tom and ask him instead could he leave the pub for an afternoon and go and see Matthew for me. James would be too busy in the fields at this time. He might be able to find out better than I would from Matthew what he would like done. Not that Matthew seems intimate with either of them. I keep up visits and invitations to them and their families because they're fine, steady, cheerful people and I think their company good for the children. "Uncles are jokey men," Margaret says, and it's well she should see plenty of jokey men. Matthew is ill at ease with them, mutters and mumbles so that they don't know what he's saying. It's peculiar that they who left school at fourteen should seem richer in themselves, more complete than Matthew, who was at school, university, and training college. We have queer ideas about education in this country; instead of looking on it as a furnishing of our minds so that we can use every room in them, we make it a ladder up the outside wall where we teeter round in every cold wind that blows.

Still, it's one of the few things in the world I'd be prepared to drop bombs about—the freedom to bring up my children with my attitude to God and people and work and money. I'd rather see them blown to bits or wasting with these diseases we hear about than systematically deprived of heaven. It would be big bombs I'd need, though, if that danger ever arose, not coal-shed hand grenades just big enough to kill or disfigure a few of the neighbors' children while they'd be playing.

I must go round the people I know in this town and impress on them that Matthew had nothing to do with endangering their children. They know he hadn't, but they might have doubts and I have none. He wouldn't

even let a broken milk bottle lie in the yard a minute longer than he could help. I have kindly feelings for Matthew when I'm lying comfortably in the middle of a cool bed, but in the daytime when I meet people I find it difficult to do more than answer their civil inquiries. I must, though, for once that's settled I've been thinking it might help Matthew to stay for a while in gaol—provided we can get something to live on.

There's an aura about people here who have been in on political charges. I was told a few years ago by a shopkeeper, "All the brave men in Ireland are in Crumlin Road gaol." He meant it too. It's dishonesty, of course. It's stealing from men who are all old now, but Matthew needs something and maybe this is the only way he can get it, although it seems shameful to me. Maybe while he's in his reputation will increase, if only in his own mind, so that he will imagine another side to his empty life as a revolutionary in a trench coat. A starving man is allowed to steal and he has shown that his real life is unbearable. It might give him a lift to come back and find himself even a little bit of a hero.

A Belfast Woman

I mind well the day the threatening letter came. It was a bright morning, and warm, and I remember thinking while I was dressing myself that it would be nice if the Troubles were over so that a body could just enjoy the feel of a good day. When I came down the stairs the hall was dark but I could see the letter lying face down. I lifted it and just my name was on the envelope, "Mrs. Harrison" in red felt pen. I knew what it was. There was a page of an exercise book inside with "Get out or we'll burn you out" all in red with bad printing and smeared. I just went in and sat at the kitchen table with the note in front of me. I never made myself a cup of tea even. It was a shock, though God knows I shouldn't have been surprised.

One of the first things I remember in my life was wakening up with my mother screaming downstairs when we were burned out in 1921. I ran down in my nightgown and my mother was standing in the middle of the kitchen with her hands up to her face screaming and screaming, and the curtains were on fire and my father was pulling them down and stamping on them with the flames catching the oilcloth on the floor. Then he shouted, "Sadie, the children," and she stopped screaming and said, "Oh, God, Michael, the children," and she ran upstairs and came down with the baby in one arm and Joey under the other, and my father took Joey in his arms and me by the hand and we ran out along the street. It was a warm summer night and the fires were crackling all over the place and the street was covered with broken glass. It wasn't until we got into my grandmother's house that anybody noticed that I had nothing on but my nightie and nothing on my feet and they were cut. It was all burned, everything they had. My mother used to say she didn't save as much as a needle and thread. I wasn't able to sleep for weeks, afraid I'd be wakened by that screaming.

We stayed in my grandmother's house until 1935 and my grandmother was dead by that time and my father too, for he got T.B. like many another then. He used to say, "When you have no house and no job sure what use are you?" and then he'd get fits of coughing. In 1935 when we got the letter threatening to burn us out I said to my mother, "We'll gather our things and we'll go." So we did, and like all the rest of them in our street we went up to Glenard to the new houses. When we showed our "Get out or we'll burn you out" note they gave us a house and we'd enough out to get things fixed up. We got new jobs in another mill, my mother and Patsy and

me. Only my mother never liked it there. She always said the air was too strong for her. It was cold right enough, up close to the mountains. But when I was getting married to William, and his aunt who was a Protestant gave him the key of her house in this street, my mother was in a terrible state—"Don't go into that Protestant street, Mary, or you'll be a sorry girl"—and she said we could live with her. But I didn't want William to pine like my poor father, so here we came and not a day's trouble until the note came.

Mind you, the second night we were here there was trouble in the Catholic streets across the road. We heard shots first and then the kind of rumbling, roaring noises of all the people out on the streets. I wanted to get up and run out and see what was wrong, but William held on to me in bed and he said, "They don't run out on the street here. They stay in." And it was true. They did. I was scared lying listening to the noise the way I never was when I was out with my neighbors. It turned out some poor young lad had stayed at home when he should have gone back to the British Army and they sent the police for him. He got out of the back window and ran down the entry and the police ran after him and shot him dead. They said their gun went off by accident but the people said they beat him up. When I went over the next day I saw him laid out in the wee room off the kitchen and his face had all big yellowy-greenish blotches on it. I never mentioned it to my new neighbors and they never mentioned it to me.

I couldn't complain about them. They were good decent people. They didn't come into the house for a chat or a loan of tea or milk or sugar like the neighbors in Glenard or North Queen Street but they were ready to help at any time. I didn't know the men much because

113

they had work so they didn't stand around the corners the way I was used to. But when Liam was born they all helped and said what a fine baby he was. He was too. Nine pounds with black hair and so strong he could lift his head and look round at a week old. They were always remarking on his mottled skin—purply kind of measles when he'd be up out of the pram—and said it was the sign of a very strong baby. At that time I had never seen a baby with any other color of skin—I suppose Catholic babies had to be strong to get by. But when Eileen was born a year and ten months later she was different. She had beautiful creamy skin. She was plump and perfect and I loved her more than Liam, God forgive me, and more than William and more than anybody in the world and I wanted everything to be right for her. I thought to myself, *If I was a Protestant now we'd have just the two and no more and I'd be able to look after them and do well for them.* So I didn't act fair with William at all.

Then I started having trouble. I looked as if I was expecting again and my stomach was hard and round but I had bleeding and I could feel no life so I was afraid. I went to the doctor and he said, "No, Mrs. Harrison, you're not pregnant. There is something here we shall have to look into." And I said, "Is it serious, doctor?" and he said, "I can't tell you that, can I, until you go into hospital and have it investigated," and I said, "Do you mean an operation?" and he said, "I do, Mrs. Harrison." I came home saying to myself, *It's cancer and who will rear my Eileen and Liam?* I remembered hearing it said that once they put the knife into you, you were dead in six months, so I made up my mind I'd have no operation and I'd last out as long as I could. Every year I was able to look after them would be a year gained and the bigger they were the better they'd be able to do without me. But

oh dear, it was terrible hard on everybody. I told William and my mother and Patsy there was nothing at all the matter with me but they knew to look at me it wasn't true. I was really wan and I was so tired I was ready to drop. I'd sit down by the fire at night when the children were in bed and my eyes would close, and if I opened them I'd see William staring at me with such a tortured look on his face I'd have to close them again so that I wouldn't go and lean my head against him and tell him the whole thing. I knew if I did that he'd make me go back to the doctor and I'd be done for. At times I'd see against my closed eyes the white long roots of the cancer growing all over my inside and I'd remember the first time William brought me to see his father in the country.

He had a fine laborer's cottage for he was a Protestant and was head plowman to some rich farmer down there. He was a good man. William's mother was a Catholic and she died when William was a wee boy but they brought him up a Catholic because it had been promised. He was cross-looking though, and I was a bit nervous of him. He had his garden all planted in rows and squares and he was digging clods in one corner and breaking them up fine and I could see all the long white roots and threads he was shaking the mud out of and he turned to us and he said, "Sitfast and scutch! Sitfast and scutch! They're the plague of my life. No matter how much I weed there's more in the morning." I told him about my grandfather and the big elderberry tree that grew behind the wee house he'd got in the country when he was burned out in Lisburn. It wasn't there when he went into the house and when he noticed it first it was only a wee bit of a bush but it grew so quickly it blocked out all the light from his back window. Then one summer it was covered with black slimy kind of flies so he cut it down to

the stump, but it started growing again straightaway. One day when my father took Patsy and Joey and me down to visit him he had dug all round the stump and he was trying to pull it out with a rope. He told my father to pull with him. My father tried but then he leaned against the wall with his face pale and covered with sweat. My grandfather said, "Are you finished, Michael?" and my father said, "I'm clean done," and my grandfather said, "God help us all," and brought us into the house and gave us lemonade. It was just after that my father went into the sanatorium and my mother was all the time bringing him bottles of lemonade. At the funeral I asked my grandfather if he got the stump out and he didn't know for a minute what I was talking about. Then he said, "No, no. Indeed the rope's still lying out there. I must bring it in or it'll rot." I never saw him again, never saw the wee house either. My mother never was one for the country.

She wasn't old herself when she died—not that much over fifty, but she looked an old woman. She wore a shawl at times and not many did that anymore. She was always fussing about my health and me going to the doctor but I managed fine without. I didn't look much. I had this swollen stomach and I got into the way of hiding it with my arms. But every year I got through I'd say to myself, wasn't I right to stick it out? When the war finished and the free health came, everybody thought I'd get myself seen to, and my mother was at me that she'd mind Liam and Eileen. Of course there were no more children but I kept those two lovely. There was no Protestant child better fed or better dressed than those two, and I always warned them to fight with nobody, never to get into trouble. If any of the children started to shout at them about being Catholics or Fenians or Teagues they

were just to walk away, not to run, mind you, but just walk home. And Liam was the best boy ever. He wasn't great at his lessons but the masters said how pleasant and good he was. Eileen was inclined to be a bit bold and that was the cause of the only terrible thing I ever did. I can't believe even now how I came to do it. It was the week after my mother had died.

I blamed myself for what happened to my mother. I should have seen in time that she wasn't well and made her mind herself and she'd have lasted better. She came into my house one day with her shawl on and I was going to say I wished she'd wear a coat and not have my neighbors passing remarks, but she hung the shawl up on the back of the door and she looked poorly. She said she'd had a terrible pain in her chest and she had been to the doctor and he'd told her it was her heart. She was to rest and take tablets. She had other wee tablets to put under her tongue if she got a pain and she was not to go up hills. She looked so bad I put her to bed in the wee room off the kitchen. She never got up again. She had tense crushing pains and the tablets did no good. Sometimes the sip of Lourdes water helped her. The doctor said he could do nothing for her unless she went into hospital and she wouldn't hear of that. "Ah no, no. I'm just done, that's all." Every now and again she'd say this would never have happened if she hadn't been burned out of her home down near the docks and had to go half roads up the mountains with all the hills and the air too strong for her. "And your father wouldn't ever have got consumption if he hadn't had to move in with my mother and spend his days at the street corner. You wouldn't remember it, Mary. You were too small," she'd say and I never contradicted her, "but we hadn't left as much as a needle and thread. The whole block went up. Nothing

left." She was buried from our house even though she kept saying she must go home. She had a horror of my Protestant neighbors even though she liked well enough the ones she met. But at her funeral, better kinder decenter neighbors you could not get. When it was over, all I could do was shiver inside myself as if my shelter had been taken away. William was good to me, always good to me, but I had to keep a bit of myself to myself with him. My mother never looked for anything from me. I'd tell her what I needed to tell her and she'd listen but she never interfered. And she was as proud of Liam and Eileen as I was. I'd see the way she looked at them.

The week after she died Eileen came home from school crying. She was ten years of age and she didn't often cry. She showed me the mark on her legs where the head teacher had hit her with a cane. A big red mark it was, right across the back of her legs. And she had lovely skin on her legs, lovely creamy skin. When I think of it I can still see that mark. I didn't ask her what happened. I just lifted my mother's shawl from where it was still hanging on the back of the kitchen door and I flung it round me and ran down to the school. I knocked on the door and she opened it herself, the head teacher, because most of the school had gone home. She took one look at me and ran away back into a classroom. I went after her. She ran into another room off it and banged the door. My arm stuck in through the glass panel and I pulled it out with a big deep cut from my wrist to my elbow. She didn't come out of the door and I never spoke to her at all. There were a couple of other teachers over a bit and a few children about but I couldn't say anything to anybody and they just stood. To stop the blood pouring so much I held my arm up out of my mother's shawl as I went back up the street. There was a woman stand-

ing at her door near the top of the street. She was gener-
ally at her door knitting, that woman. She had very
clever children and some of them did well. One got to be
a teacher; another was in the post office, which is about
as far as a clever poor Catholic can get. She asked me
what happened but when I couldn't answer she said,
"You'd need to get to the hospital, missus, I'll get my
coat and go with you." I didn't want to go to any hospital. I just wanted to go home and wash off all the blood
but my head was spinning so I let myself be helped on
the bus. They stitched it up and wanted me to stay in for
the night but I was terrified they'd operate on me just
when I was managing so well. I insisted I couldn't because the children were on their own and Mrs. O'Reilly
came with me right to the end of my own street. "If your
neighbors ask what happened, just tell them you fell off
the bus," she told me. "You don't want them knowing all
about your business." I've heard she was from the west
of Ireland.

When I went into the kitchen I was ready to drop but
Eileen started screaming and crying and saying how
ashamed of me she was and that she'd never go back to
school again. Liam made me a cup of tea and stood looking worried at me. When William came in from work he
helped me to bed and was kind and good but I could see
by the cut of his mouth that he was shocked and of-
fended at me. It took a long time to heal and the scar will
never leave me. The story went around the parish in different ways. Some said I hit the teacher. Some said she
knifed me. I was too ashamed ever to explain.

Eileen never was touched in school after that, though,
and when she left she learned shorthand and typing and
got an office job. She grew up lovely, and I used to think,
watching her going out in the morning in the best of

119

clothes with her hair shining, that she could have gone anywhere and done herself credit. She wasn't contented living where we did. At first I didn't understand what she wanted. I thought she wanted a better house in a better district. I didn't know how we could manage it but I made up my mind it would have to be done. I went for walks up round the avenues where there were detached houses with gardens and when I saw an empty house I'd peer in through the windows. Then one day a woman from the parish, who worked cleaning one of those houses, saw me and asked me in because the people of the house were out all day. Seeing it furnished with good solid shining furniture I knew we'd never manage it. In the sitting room there was an old-fashioned copper canopy over the fire and when I looked into it I could see the whole room reflected smaller like a fairy tale with flowers and books and pictures and plates on the wall. I knew it wasn't for us. How could I go in and out there? William and Liam wouldn't look right in their working clothes. Only Eileen would fit in. I was a bit sad but relieved because at no time could I see where the money would have come from. I told her that night when she came in but she looked at me all puzzled. "But that wasn't what I meant, Mammy," she said. "I have to get away from everything here. There's no life for me here. I'm thinking of going to Canada." That was before any trouble at all here. People now would say that was in the good times when you could get in a bus and go round the shops or into the pictures and nothing would have happened by the time you came home except that the slack would have burned down a bit on the fire.

Off she went anyway and got a job and wrote now and again telling us how well off she was. In no time at all she was married and was sending photographs, first

of this lovely bungalow and then of her two wee girls with the paddling pool in her garden or at their swing when they were a bit bigger. I was glad she was doing so well. It was the kind of life I had reared her for and dreamed of for her, only I wished she and her children were not so far away. I kept inviting her home for a visit but I knew it would cost far too much money. Only I thought if she was homesick it would help her to know we wanted to see her too. Once the troubles came I stopped asking her.

Liam at that time was getting on well too. He was always such a nice pleasant big fellow that a plumber in the next street to ours asked him to join in his business at putting in fireplaces and hot-water pipes. Liam put in a lovely fireplace for me with a copper canopy like the one I'd seen years before and built me a bathroom and hot water and put in a sink unit for me till I was far better off than any of my neighbors, even though a lot of them had their houses very nice too. They were able to get paint from the shipyard of course, and marble slabs and nice bits of mahogany. He got married to a nice wee girl from the Bone and they got a house up in one of the nice streets in Ardoyne—up the far end in what they call now a mixed area. It's all gone, poor Liam's good way of living. When that street of houses up there was put on fire in 1972 his wife Gemma insisted on coming back to the Bone and squatting in an empty house. They did their best to fix it up but it's old and dark. Then when the murders got bad his partner asked him not to come back to work anymore because he'd been threatened for working with a Catholic. I was raging when Liam told me, raging about what a coward the plumber was, but then as Liam said, you can't blame a man for not wanting to be murdered. So there he is—no work and no house and

a timid wife and a family of lovely wee children. He had plenty to put up with. But where else could I go when I got the note? I sat looking round my shining kitchen and the note said, "Get out or we'll burn you out," and where could I go for help but to Liam?

Still I was glad William was dead before it happened. He would have been so annoyed. He felt so ashamed when the Protestants did something nasty. I could swallow my own shame every time the I.R.A. disgraces us. I lived with it the same as I lived with the memory of my own disgrace when I went for the teacher and ripped my arm. But William had always been such a good upright man, he could never understand wickedness. Even the way he died showed it. He was a carter all his days, always in steady work, but for a while before he died they were saying to him that nobody had horses anymore and they were changing to a lorry. He could never drive a lorry. He was afraid he'd be on the dole. It wasn't the money he was worrying about, for I kept telling him it would make little difference to us—just the two of us, what did it matter? It was his pride that was upset. For years there was a big notice up on a corner shop at the bottom of the Oldpark Road. It said, "Drivers, dismount. Don't overload your horses going up the hill." He used to remark on it. It irked him if he didn't obey it. So one day in March when there was an east wind he collapsed on the hill and died the next day in hospital with the same disease as my mother.

There was a young doctor in the hospital asked me did I need a tranquilizer or a sleeping tablet or something to get over the shock. I told him no, that I never took any tablets, that I had had cancer when I was in my twenties and that I was still alive in my fifties with never a day in bed. He was curious and he asked me questions and then

he said, "Mrs. Harrison, of course I can't be absolutely sure, but I'd say it was most unlikely you had cancer. Maybe you needed a job done on your womb. Maybe you even needed your womb removed but I would be very, very surprised if you had cancer. You wouldn't be here now if you had." So I went in and knelt down at William's side. He still had that strained, worried look, even then. All I could think was: *Poor William. Poor William. Poor, poor, poor William.*

It wasn't that I was lonely without him for I'd kept him at a distance for a long time, but the days had no shape to them. I could have my breakfast, dinner, and tea whatever time I liked or I needn't have them at all. For a while I didn't bother cooking for myself, just ate tea and bread. Then Liam's wife, Gemma, said the butcher told her that I hadn't darkened his door since William died and that if I wouldn't cook for myself I'd have to come and have my dinner with them. So I thought to myself I wasn't being sensible and I'd only be a nuisance to them if I got sick, so I fixed everything to the clock as if there was no such thing as eternity. Until that morning the note came and then I just sat; I didn't know how long I stayed. I felt heavy, not able to move. Then I thought maybe Liam could get somebody with a van to take out my furniture and I could think later where to go. I took my rosary beads from under my pillow and my handbag with my money and my pension book and Eileen's letters and the photographs of her children and I shut the door behind me. There wasn't a soul in the street but there was nothing odd about that. You'll always know you're in a Protestant street if it's deserted. When I went across the road to get to Liam's house there were children playing and men at the corner and women standing at the

doors in the sun and a squad of nervous-looking soldiers down at the other end.

Liam wasn't in but Gemma and the children were. The breakfast table wasn't cleared and Gemma was feeding the youngest. When he finished she stood him up on her lap and he reached over her shoulder trying to reach the shiny new handle Liam had put on the door. He was sturdy and happy and he had a warm smell of milk and baby powder. I wanted to hold him but I was afraid of putting her out of her routine. Sometimes I wonder if she has a routine—compared to the way I reared mine. Nothing was allowed to interrupt their feeding times and sleeping times. Maybe I was wrong and I'll never know what way Eileen managed hers. I would have liked to do the dishes too but I was afraid it might look like criticizing. After a wee while chatting Gemma got up to put the child in his pram and make us a cup of tea. "You don't look great, Granny," she said. "Are you minding yourself at all?" I opened my bag and showed her the note.

She screamed and put her hands up to her face and the baby was startled and cried and bounced up and down in his pram with his arms up to be lifted. I said, "Don't scream, Gemma. Don't ever scream, do you hear me?" and I unstrapped the baby and hugged him. She stared at me, surprised, and it stopped her.

"You'll have to come and stay here," she said. "We'll fit you in." She gave a kind of a look round and I could see her thinking where on earth she could fit me in. Still, where could I go?

"All I wanted was for Liam to get a van and take out my stuff," I explained. "Maybe my sister Patsy would have more room than you."

She took the baby and gave me my cup of tea. "You'll come here," she said. "You'll count this your home and

we'll be glad to have you." She was a good kind girl, Gemma, and when Liam came in he was the same, only anxious to make me welcome, and he went off to get the van.

After a while Gemma said, "Write to Eileen straight-away. She's the one you should be living with anyway—not all alone over yonder. All her money and her grand house. She's the one should have you."

I laughed but it hurt me a bit to hear it said. "What would I do in Eileen's grand house in Canada? How would I fit in?"

And Gemma said, "You could keep her house all shining. She'd use you for that. Where would you see the like of your own house for polish! You'd do great for Eileen." I looked round her own few bits and pieces—no look on anything, and a pile of children's clothes on the floor waiting to be washed and the children running in and out and knocking things over. Mary, my wee god-child, came and stood leaning against my knees, sucking her thumb. She was wearing one of the dresses I make for them. In the spring when I was fitting it on her I was noticing how beautiful her skin was with little pinprick freckles on the pink and white and I was thinking, *When she's so lovely what must Eileen's children be like?* Then she turned her head and looked at me and her eyes were full of love—for me! I couldn't get over it. Since then some-times she'd just hold my hand. When Liam came back I said, "Liam, I'm going home. I'm sorry about the bother. I just got frightened but you can cancel the van. I'm going home and I'm staying home. I've a Protestant house to the right of me and a Protestant house to the left of me. They'll not burn me out." They argued with me and they were a bit upset but I knew they were relieved and I stuck to it.

Liam insisted on going back to the house with me, although since the murders started I had never let him come down my side of the road. There was a Land-Rover with soldiers in it not far from my door and no flames, no smoke. But when I opened the door, such a mess. There was water spouting out of a broken pipe in the wall where they had pulled out my sink. The Sacred Heart statute and the wee red lamp were broken on the floor. My copper canopy was all dinged. The table had big hatchet marks on it. The cover on the couch was ripped and the stuffing pulled out. And filth. For months I thought I could get the smell of that filth. I wouldn't let Liam turn off the water until I had it washed away. We cleaned up a bit but Liam said he'd have to get help before he could do much and not to touch the electric because the water had got into it. He had been very quiet so I jumped when he shouted at the soldiers once he went out the door. They drove up very slowly and he was shouting and waving his arms and calling them names. One of them looked into the house and started to laugh. Liam yelled at him about me being a widow woman living alone and that they were here to protect me, but one of them said, "You've got it wrong. We're here to wipe out the I.R.A."

"Oh, Liam," I said, "go home. Go home before harm befalls you," and he shook his fist at the soldiers and shouted, "I'm going now but I'll be back and I won't be on my own then. Just look out. I'm warning you."

He turned and ran off down the street and the soldier turned and looked after him and I thought he was lifting up his gun and I grabbed at his arm and the gun went off into the air and I begged, "Don't shoot at him. Oh, don't shoot him."

He said, "Missus, I have no intention . . ." and then I

fell against the wall and when I came to they were making me drink whiskey out of a bottle. It made me cough and splutter but it brought me round. They weren't bad to me, I must admit. When I was on my feet they corked up the bottle and put it back in the Land-Rover and drove off. Not one of my neighbors came out and all evening when I worked at tidying up, and all night when I sat up to keep watch, not one of them knocked at my door.

Next day Liam brought back two other lads and they fixed up the electricity and the water. It took a while to get everything decent again but they were in and out every day, sometimes three or four of them, and it never cost me a penny. Then a queer thing happened. My neighbors began moving out. The woman next door told me out of the side of her mouth that they had all been threatened. I didn't understand how a whole Protestant area could be threatened but out they all went. Of course I know they can always get newer better houses when they ask for them and indeed there was a lot of shooting and wrecking on the front of the road, but still I often wondered what was the truth of it. Maybe I'm better off not knowing. As they left, Catholics from across the road moved in—mostly older people—and I have good friends among them although it took us a while to get used to each other. I didn't take easy to people expecting to open my door and walk in at any hour of the day. They thought I was a bit stiff. I have no time for long chats and I never liked gossip. But Mrs. Mulvenna, next door now, has a son in Australia—farther away than my Eileen and I think sons are even worse at writing home. I listen to her and I feel for her and I show her my photographs. I didn't tell her when Eileen wrote about how ashamed she was of us all and how she didn't like to let

on she was Irish. I see talk like that in the papers too. It's not right to put the blame on poor powerless people. The most of us never did anything but stay quiet and put up with things the way they were. And we never taught our children to hate the others nor filled their heads with their wrongs the way it's said we did. When all the young people thought they could fix everything with marches and meetings I said it wouldn't work and they laughed at me. "All you old ones are awful bitter," they said and they jeered when Hannah in the shop and I were warning them, "It'll all lead to shooting and burning and murder."

Still, last November a man came round here trying to sell venetian blinds. Some of the houses have them but I said no, I liked to see out. I pointed to the sunset behind Divis—bits of red and yellow in the sky and a sort of mist all down the mountain that made it nearly see-through. The man looked at it for a minute and then he said, "Do you know Belfast has the most beautiful sunsets in the whole world?" I said I didn't because I'd never been anyplace else to look at sunsets and he said, "They tell me Belfast has the best and do you know why? It's because of all the smoke and dirt and dust and pollution. And it seems to me," he said, "it seems to me that if the dirt and dust and smoke and pollution of Belfast just with the help of the sun can make a sky like that, then there's hope for all of us." He nodded and winked and touched his hat and went off and I went in and sat down at the table. And thinking of it I started to laugh, for it's true. There is hope for all of us. Well, anyway, if you don't die you live through it, day in, day out.

Failing Years

Nora sat tense in the upright chair she used nowadays until her daughter banged the door behind her without saying goodbye. Then she went to the front window and watched as Una eased herself into her car. She wished she had not snapped at her. But Una so seldom left the house for any length of time that when she said she'd be away until teatime, and then fussed, upstairs and down, giving directions about the fire and the lunch, Nora could bear the delay no longer and said, "Una, I can manage without you. I am not a fool. And it *is* my house."

She felt no kinship with this sedate, solid, middle-aged woman. She tried to remember the slim, lively girl who had been such a delight to Alec and herself. She was

the eldest of the family and Alec and Nora had congratulated each other while she was growing up that no matter what bother they had with the four boys who came after her, they never had to trouble about Una. They had been completely taken aback by her unsuitable marriage. Why should she have married before she was twenty a man so old for her? His stiff, polite manner to her parents seemed a continual reproach. When he died eventually, Nora wondered what sympathy she should feel for her daughter. "It was not," she said to Alec, "as if it was a real marriage, like ours." Alec had looked doubtful and had worried about Una alone, growing fat, but Nora had never felt welcome in that big, pompous house with the heavy blinds at the windows, so she expected no support from Una when Alec himself died suddenly.

He had been retired for some years, the family was gone, and Nora and he were very happy together in the routine they made for themselves. Then the night after he had got injections for varicose veins he had been restless, and she worried about him. The next morning was a First Friday and they decided to walk to Mass, since the doctor had told him to use his legs instead of his car. Just inside the church he fell full length on his back. "Poleaxed"—the word sat in her mind. The priest rushed to give him the last rites. They sent for an ambulance. Some woman whispered, "Such a fine figure of a man." Nora knew he was dead. She stood looking at his high color fade and his white shining hair seemed to lose its vitality while she watched. She had often said to him that it would be nice if his car would go out of control and smash into a wall and kill the both of them and not leave one lonely. Now he was gone and she was left waiting. Of course he had gone off and left her waiting many a time on his trips abroad, but then she knew he'd be back

with a present for her and a suitcase full of dirty clothes. She'd often thought, as the smell of exotic cigarettes and strange rooms rose out of the washing machine, that that was her share of the foreign travel. She had never been out of Ireland. He promised that they would go when he retired, but she had been afraid of the effort it would have meant for both of them. They used to do shopping sometimes in Dun Laoire on sunny summer Fridays, and watching the big white ferry and the sharp blue sea and the painted terraces, she used to say, "Isn't this as good as the South of France any day?" Now he was gone for good. At first she couldn't sleep, and when she mentioned that, they gave her sleeping tablets. So she slept sound and wakened in the morning feeling the empty half of the bed, wondering, *How could he be up without my noticing?* and then, remembering, felt such a heaviness in her chest that she decided sleeplessness was preferable any time.

She began to feel old. For years before Alec died she had noticed casually the signs of age. When she looked in the mirror with her glasses on she was disgusted, so she took off her glasses and smiled at the improvement. She had always made the effort to keep her shoulders straight, and when she was able to buy expensive clothes her long, thin figure looked elegant, but most of her life she could only afford cheaper ones. Her sisters in Belfast sometimes presented her with things to wear. Alec always told her she looked well. She thought it didn't mean a thing to her because he did not discriminate. But with him gone there was no one to praise her, no one to laugh at her, no one to touch her.

Fending for herself, her main trouble was the new range in the kitchen. All her married life she had lamented the lack of her mother's black, burnished range

in the three-story terrace house where she had been reared in Belfast. The bread baked in it was so much better than anything she could produce in her electric cooker. It had heated the water so well that on winter evenings the whole house rumbled and shook with the vibrations of the boiler. So when Alec retired and he had time to listen to her, he had a modern range installed. He took great satisfaction in stoking it, praising its warmth and everything Nora cooked on it. Nora didn't feel it was as good as the fires of her childhood when the glow behind the bars had been a dangerous delight, but she joined in Alec's praises with gratitude. Now she had difficulty with it. She had not the strength in her hands to riddle it properly, so that ash prevented it burning as brightly as it should. The ash pan was so heavy she needed two hands to lift it and so had nothing to lean on to help herself off her knees. She didn't complain, even to herself, because she had a fear that if she did, it would postpone Alec's happiness in the next world. Summers were easier. She cooked and cleaned and shopped and visited the two sons who were married in Dublin and wrote letters to the two who were away. She chatted with the neighbors and because she had lived there so long the familiar faces were a strength to her—until she too fell in the church.

It was Sunday and the church was crowded, so she was waiting to kneel at the altar rail when the whole sanctuary turned copper color and then purple so that she staggered and sat back on the seat behind her. She could hear the voice of the priest: "Body of Christ, Body of Christ," but she couldn't see, and she thought she was going to die and felt terror. Somebody helped her out of the church and after Mass drove her home. A neighbor telephoned for Una, who insisted she'd had a stroke and

that it would be necessary for her to move into the house. Nora said, such nonsense, it was only chapel sickness, other people suffered it frequently, but of course Una could come and stay if she wished to. And before she had really collected herself Una's house was sold, the money was in the bank, and Una was in charge. When the neighbors called to welcome Una back it was Una who had their sympathy. When they asked Nora how she felt, she was cross—"I am perfectly well"—but sometimes she worried. She had difficulty with words. She noticed it first when some of her grandchildren came in the summer and she cut up a block of ice cream and asked them to pass her the rashers instead of the wafers. She had to laugh with them at how stupid Granny was. A few days later she asked in a shop for coconut twist instead of buttonhole twist. Sometimes she couldn't think of the words she wanted at all and her tongue felt heavy in her mouth.

Anxiety kept her lying awake at night. Before Una moved in she hadn't really minded waking up in the night. She switched on her lamp and read a book, or went downstairs and sat drinking tea while she read. Now she had to lie still or Una was up inquiring what was wrong, was she all right, when would she go back to bed, when would she put out her light, would she have a sleeping tablet? It was easier to stay quiet. She remembered the advice she had always given to children wakening from nightmares—"Think of something pleasant." So she thought of the security of that warm house in Belfast with her own energetic mother who had never completely reconciled herself to town life. During school holidays she had often gathered up her children and taken them down to the farm near the shores of Lough Neagh where she had been reared. There they tore

through the fields, slid down haystacks, rode on the ruck shifter, and ran in and out of the drafty stone-flagged kitchen to take turns at the clackety wheel of the fan-bellows blazing the fire up the wide chimney so that her grandmother feared for the thatch. Coming back there was the excitement of the pony and trap tilting downhill and up so that Nora was afraid she'd fall out over the pony's head, or back against her stout grandfather, of whom they were all nervous. The road ran between orchards with the trunks whitewashed so that they stood in the evening like neat, well-ordered ghosts. Nora was glad of the safety of trains and trams, and even her mother when she entered her own cluttered, red-papered hall used to say, "Well, we had a great day but it's not bad to be home."

"Well, now I've the house to myself," Nora said aloud after Una's car had disappeared. She moved from room to room taking possession, enjoying the freedom. She came back into the kitchen heated by the range well lit and smiled with pleasure in the warmth of the November sun on her legs.

She could not relax with Una in the house, whether she was in the same room with her or not. Una's ways filled her with impatience. She tried to contain it but often she heard herself speaking irritably, criticizing what Una was doing. Una then went about for long hours in an awkward silence. She put the transistor on the table between them at mealtimes. Nora tried to make conversation in spite of it. She tried to talk about what she thought might interest Una. Una looked at her blankly, as if what she was saying did not make sense. Maybe it didn't. Una had bought brown plates for everyday use to save her mother's good china. On the brown were black, skeletal birds top and bottom, intertwined, with big bills

meeting and eyes staring. There was no expression in those eyes but they menaced Nora. She thought Alec would have managed Una far better. At the time of his death she had consoled herself that it was better for him to go first than be left helpless, but now with Una in the house he would not have been unhappy at all. Alec and Una might have enjoyed life without her quite well.

She took the meat for her lunch from the fridge and looked at it with distaste. "We'll have a tea-dinner," her mother used to announce long ago whenever there were no men or boys to cater for, and they would be treated to an omelet or pancakes or potato bread with caraway seeds and then one of the hot, sugary things her mother made with apples. They grew apples in the long garden behind the house. Nora used to climb one of the trees and sit contentedly in it eating the small green apples that the others scorned. Once she fell down on a wooden box with a nail that tore the top of her leg. She went in sore and frightened and was told to put iodine on it. As she sat on the sofa in the kitchen dabbing at it, she found a pea-sized lump of her flesh separate and she lifted it out, pink and solid. She held it up, asking what she would do with it, and her mother gasped, "Oh, Nora, put it in the fire," but her brother shouted, "No, no, we must have a funeral," and they put it in a little matchbox and dug a hole in the garden and buried it. Then they stood around, feeling something else was necessary, but they had never been at a funeral. "We'll sing 'Nearer by God to Thee,'" Nora suggested. Their father had said that somebody he knew called Johnnie Donnelly had told him that on the *Titanic* before it went down they'd all sung 'Nearer by God to Thee,' and her parents had laughed and then said, "It's not right to be laughing." The children couldn't understand the joke as they had

never heard the hymn. They didn't know the tune either, so they just shouted the words over and over into the golden September garden and Nora came in feeling much better. Her mother, dressing it daily, marveled that the ugly scar was exactly the shape of Lough Neagh.

Nora's own apple trees were neglected, the branches green and straggling. Alec had planted them for her when she came to live in Dublin. He had pruned them and sprayed them. At Hallow Eve he had picked off the Bramleys, apple by apple, and sorted them according to size in three or four boxes to keep Nora supplied until Easter. The autumn after his death two of her sons came with their children and Nora's heart had warmed watching them do as Alec had done, and listening to them laughing. Then it appeared that they were dividing them evenly between themselves with one small box for her. Of course she would have given them the apples, but she would have liked to *have* the giving of them. They would never have treated Alec like that. She was annoyed because she felt such resentment. Very early in her marriage she had made up her mind never to resent anything and had disciplined herself to keep to that. Now she felt resentment again as she looked for something interesting to have with her "tea-dinner." There were no scones, no cake, no tart, no home-baked bread even, because Una was slimming and believed that if there was no food to tempt her she would lose weight. But Nora had seen her many times eating bars of chocolate after a meager lunch. All her life Nora had taken great satisfaction in well-stocked cupboards. Now the presses were empty.

The house in Belfast was empty too. The last time Nora had visited her sisters she had gone to see the old house and found it bricked up, inaccessible. An army car drove past slowly with two bored soldiers in the back,

their guns pointing down the road. The pub at the corner was burned out, its pitted brick blackened and the pavement shattered. Nora had been in that pub only once. She had been seventeen and running home from a friend's house at curfew time when shots rattled in the next street. A man pulled her into the pub and shut the door behind her. He was young and a stranger. The only other person there was the middle-aged barman, whom she knew by sight. He looked annoyed. "Aren't you a young Magee from up the road? What in the name of God are you doing out after the curfew?" She couldn't make herself answer. She was shivering. She was completely out of place. Then the young man in the raincoat smiled at her and she felt deep inside her the beginning of something almost like laughter. When they checked that the road was clear she slipped home, and while her harassed parents scolded her she was looking at herself smiling in the oval, oak-framed mirror in the red hall. For years that smiling face occupied her daydreams. Even after she was married to Alec it was not entirely obliterated. Sometimes at night while he was asleep and she lay worrying if Una was warm enough in bed or if Andy's cough would ever clear up, she would close her eyes and the disembodied smile would taunt her.

Now looking out at the pale sun shining through the cypresses at the end of the garden, she suddenly decided she would go to Belfast and she began to tremble with excitement. There was a train at half past five—there was always the *Enterprise* at half past five. She had plenty of time to catch it. She rang a taxi—she was still good at remembering numbers—and went upstairs to get ready. She was going only for a visit to her sisters, she told herself. It didn't matter that the house was gone. She'd meet all her old friends and have great evenings by the fire,

137

talking. She'd listen to all the gossip even if she couldn't remember the people, and relish the old jokes and the occasional spurt of venom. She had to look well, going up. She put on her good winter coat and her fur hat. There had been a row with Una over buying that hat. It cost twenty-seven pounds and Una had held up her hands in horror but Nora bought it. "Your father always liked me to have a fur hat to keep my head warm." And when Una insisted that the price was exorbitant, she retorted, "You say yourself money has no value anymore." Her bag and gloves were years old but still good, she thought, as she settled back happily into the corner of the taxi.

"You'll love Dublin," Alec had told her when they got married. "We'll have great times there." But she had not loved Dublin. She had been lonely and homesick, totally dependent on Alec for comfort. It had been many years before she became accustomed to the strange streets and difficult distances. In the crowds downtown she never met by chance a familiar face. And the arrival of one child after the other finished any possibility of "great times." Then one St. Patrick's Night a neighbor insisted on baby-sitting for them. It was too late to book for a play and when they went into town the restaurants and cinemas were all full, so they strolled around arm in arm looking at shopwindows. It was a mild night and hundreds of other people were doing the same. Nora became aware of a light, bubbling sound rising from the streets and she realized it was people laughing all over the town. So she began to have an affection for Dublin as one can grow fond of someone else's child.

She paid the taximan outside the station. "My case?" she said.

"You hadn't got any case," he said and then looked

concerned. "Did you forget it? We'd never make it back again in time." She was confused but assured him she was quite all right without it. At the ticket office she was told, "This train only travels to Dundalk."

"But I want to buy a second-class return for Belfast," she repeated.

"Bus connections to Portadown," the man said impatiently and she drew her money back out again, murmuring she'd better think about it. She stopped a uniformed railway man who was limping in a hurry over to the *Enterprise* gate and asked him to explain.

"You get the train to Dundalk, ma'am, buses to Portadown, and train again to Belfast. It's a long old journey. Tiresome."

"But what can be the reason?" she asked.

"Bombs along the line, ma'am. That's it. Bombs along the line."

"But I thought they'd stopped all that," she said.

"Sure, didn't we all. But they've started again. There y'are." He went off but came back in a moment to find her still standing there. He assured her, "If you have to get home to Belfast, ma'am, we'll get you there all right. Only it'll be a bit longsome."

"Oh, no," she said, "my home is in Dublin."

"Ah, well then, you're all right. I'd get back there then and ring up your friends in Belfast and tell them you're not coming. They'll know what it's like."

"How will I get home?" she asked helplessly.

"You'll get a bus at the foot of the steps there." He pointed. "Can you manage the steps?"

"Of course I can," she said indignantly and started off urgently, hoping to get home before Una. But no bus came until she was frozen and despairing. She looked round for support and saw another woman waiting in

the shelter of the wall. She was perhaps not as old as Nora but she was poor and bent, in a shapeless coat and thin headscarf.

"Oh, isn't the buses brutal?" she sighed and Nora agreed.

"The trains too."

"I didn't know there was anything wrong with the trains," the woman said. "But then it's years and years since I was on a train. Not since I used to bring the children to the seaside." She laughed. "They were great days. I used to pack all the picnic and bathing things in the bottom of the pram—do you remember the big deep prams there were then?—and wheel them down to the station here with the smallest two in the pram and the others holding on at the sides. But sure they're only lent to you. Isn't that true?"

"Do you live with any of your children?" Nora asked.

"I do not," she said. "Since *he* died I've the pension myself. I have my independence. It's a great thing to have."

Eventually arriving home to find lights on all over the house, she determined she would say nothing of where she had been. Her cold fingers had difficulty turning the key in the lock and before she could manage, Una flung open the door, her face anxious, her voice sharp, harassing her mother with questions. Nora said, "If you don't mind, Una, I'm going straight up to bed. I am very, very tired." She leaned against the wall to rest her legs and in the bright hall the unframed mirror reflected a wrinkled, powdery face with a wisp of gray hair untidy on the forehead. She looked down to the hall table where the big blue-and-white jug Dermot had brought her home years ago from some student trip held the white chrysanthemums slightly browned at the under edges. She

didn't like white chrysanthemums. They reminded her too much of funerals—real, unhappy funerals. She remembered, fleetingly, daffodils covering banks at the side of the road and the corner of a field, escaped probably from some big house.

"The flowers are withered, Una," she said. "We must buy different ones tomorrow."

"But where did you go?" Una repeated. "What did you think I'd feel coming home to find the house in darkness and the fire out and you not here?"

"I'm sorry it was uncomfortable for you, Una," Nora apologized sarcastically. "You haven't managed to warm up the house much yet."

"How could I?" Una demanded. "I've been on the phone to everybody I knew to find out where you were. You went off in a taxi?"

"I did," Nora answered. "Thank God I have a little money left to save me from hardship."

"Oh, Mother," Una said, "why do you say such things?"

Why indeed? Nora wondered to herself as she went slowly upstairs. Una followed her into her bedroom and stood looking at her uncertainly while she struggled to open her hot-water bottle. She could not unscrew the cap. Una said she would go down and ring her brothers to tell them their mother was safely home. "I'd like you to fill my bottle first," Nora had to ask. "You need be in no hurry ringing Andy or Donal. They don't care what happens to me."

"Mother, are you out of your mind?" Una exclaimed. Nora sat down on the stool at her dressing table, huddled in her good coat and fur hat until the electric heater had taken the chill off the room. "Will you have a hot bath?" Una asked, coming back.

"I don't think I could," her mother answered.

"Will I get the doctor for you then?"

"Indeed you will not. What good would the doctor do? I'm beginning to warm now, but I'm hungry."

"Hungry?" Una echoed.

"I haven't had a thing to eat since morning," Nora began and then shut her lips tight. When Una was gone she undressed in a hurry, leaving her clothes untidily on the stool but taking her handbag within reach on the bedside table. There were warm spots in the bed but most of it was so cold it felt damp.

She would never let them know where she'd gone, she repeated to herself. It was something of her own to hold on to. Then she realized that if she was very careful and kept Una at bay, Belfast would still be there for her. She would try again sometime in the spring, when the weather was warmer or the Troubles were over. She was afraid, though, it would all come out somehow, some way or another, during the dark enclosed days.

M000195441